MW00526306

Surviving Wisdom

to Carrol & Red —
With All Best Wishes

Surviving Wisdom

Ken Hodgson

Ken Hodgson

April 19 2006

Five Star • Waterville, Maine

Copyright © 2003 by Ken Hodgson

All rights reserved.

This novel is a work of fiction. Names, characters, places and incidents are either the product of the author's imagination, or, if real, used fictitiously.

First Edition
First Printing: July 2003

Published in 2003 in conjunction with Tekno Books and Ed Gorman.

Set in 11 pt. Plantin by Ramona A. Watson.

Printed in the United States on permanent paper.

Library of Congress Cataloging-in-Publication Data

Hodgson, Ken.
Surviving wisdom / Ken Hodgson.—1st ed.
p. cm
ISBN 0-7862-5437-8 (hc : alk. paper)
1. World War, 1939–1945—New Mexico—Fiction.
2. Murder for hire—Fiction. 3. New Mexico—Fiction.
4. Arson—Fiction. I. Title.
PS3558.O34346S87 2003
813′.6—dc21 2003052920

This book is for
Loren D. Estleman

ACKNOWLEDGEMENTS

I wish to thank Ed Gorman, Russell Davis, Deborah Brod, and John Helfers for making it happen.

I owe special thanks to my wife, Rita, for endless hours of typing and editing.

The friendly people of Silver City, New Mexico were most helpful in researching the rich history of that area.

AUTHOR'S NOTE

Historians and those familiar with the State of New Mexico will quickly note that I have modeled my fictional town of Wisdom on the real-life village of Mogollon, which, though it came close, never became a true ghost town.

The government did order the closing of all gold mines in 1942, relegating many remote hamlets to the pages of history books. I have often pondered what life must have been like for the few who stayed on in such places, clinging to their dreams. I can only hope I did them justice. Angel's Roost Mountain is a product of my imagination, as are all of the characters in this book, save a few historical personages which I have used fictionally.

Ken Hodgson
San Angelo, Texas, 2002

Wisdom crieth without; she uttereth her voice in the street.

Proverbs I.20

Disappointment is the nurse of wisdom.

Sir Boyle Roche

CHAPTER ONE

October 1942

"That house of yours is burning down good enough to send up quite a smoke signal. I'd reckon even Slow Ron will have to take notice of it fairly soon."

Woody Johnson lowered the binoculars from his gray eyes and turned to his friend, Pat Gunn, as he walked out onto the squeaking plank porch of the pallid log cabin that clung tenuously to the craggy cliffs high on Angel's Roost Mountain overlooking the town of Wisdom, New Mexico.

Pat swirled his glass of whiskey and smiled with satisfaction at the tinkling sound. "Hailstones make the world's best ice for scotch. I'm glad you saved some from that last storm."

"They didn't cost nothing," Woody said. "God tossed 'em at me for free." He squinted down through the haze of a gossamer white cloud being driven by on the always-present wind and frowned. "I hope like heck that house of yours don't catch the whole town afire. There's still a bar and cathouse down there that's worth saving."

"I'm more worried about Slow Ron getting lucky and putting the fire out before there's nothing left to save." Pat took a sip of whiskey, stepped to the pole railing and studied the streets of the town that sprawled like a tattered spiderweb in the sinuous canyons a quarter mile below. "When the Elliots' house burned, Ron saved enough of their place that the insurance company built it back. I can't afford to have something like that happen."

"No, I'd reckon that would be a heck of a thing. With the gold mines closed and all the young folks either moved away or gone to war, a house in Wisdom ain't worth a fart in a whirlwind, only you don't have to pay taxes on farts, at least not yet. But once those damn tax-happy bastards—"

The distant wail of a siren brought Woody's tirade to an end. In a remote mountain town where most of the buildings had been hastily constructed of wood during a decades-past gold rush, the howl of a fire alarm brought every able-bodied person out to fight the flames before a conflagration wiped the entire town from the map.

In Wisdom, New Mexico, however, the population had plummeted from nearly three thousand souls in the spring of the year to around thirty hopefuls who still hung on, clinging to dreams; or they were simply old and had been living here so long they couldn't conceive of any other place to go to. Everything here was as familiar and comfortable as a pair of old shoes.

Pat grabbed up Woody's binoculars. "Well, from the looks of things, Slow Ron's got the fire truck started. Joe Godfrey and Fred Chapman's climbing on. They'll most likely squirt what water they've got on those abandoned shacks next to my place to keep the fire from spreading. The nearest hydrant's too far away for them to run a line. With decent luck all I'll have left when I get down there is a smoldering foundation."

"Ron's well noted for never losing a foundation."

"Then I'll call my insurance agent in Silver City and have him come up and give me a check for three grand. Not a bad deal since I couldn't sell that house for a hundred bucks."

"I reckon." Woody snorted and took a sack of Bull Durham from his jacket pocket. He slipped a thin paper from a packet, then creased it into a V and shook it full of tobacco with a practiced motion. "You still planning on living in that room back of your moving picture theater?"

"The Starlight's all I have left. I figure with the insurance money I can hang on for quite some time and maybe even show a movie once in a while. This war won't last much longer; then the government will lift that moratorium they issued on mining gold. Wisdom will boom again, you can bet on it."

"General Doolittle sure bombed those gooks' nest in Tokyo this spring." Woody finished rolling his cigarette and took a moment to fire it before continuing. "But my guess is this darn war will go on for at least another year or so. That German paper hanger, Adolf Hitler, is still putting up a real scrap in Europe. Add in Mussolini, along with the Japs, and it causes a major inconvenience to all of us over here. First the Japs bomb Pearl Harbor and all the young'uns run to join the Army. Then the government orders the gold mines closed to make the miners only mine lead and such."

"And the mines here in Wisdom only produced gold."

"That's a fact, Pat, but that government of ours and their regulations went and put a world of hurt on a lot of towns like Wisdom. If the war drags on much longer, the mines will flood or cave in. Then it'll cost a fortune to open them up again."

"A year or so is all it will be," Pat said hopefully. "By then you might even have found ore here in this mine of yours."

"Three more feet is all," Woody said with certainty. "I've finally got the mother lode doodlebugged out. I can't believe how I managed to miss it before."

Pat Gunn took a swig of scotch to disguise a sigh. Old Woody had spent the past twenty-seven years living on this wind-blown cliff, driving tunnels willy-nilly in pursuit of an ever-elusive vein. The man, using mostly worn out machinery and working alone, had punched nearly a half-mile hole inside Angel's Roost Mountain. By most measurements he would come out the other side fairly soon. Woody's faith never wavered, even though he had yet to find enough gold to fill a bad tooth and was forced to tend bar or chop wood for money to buy beans, tobacco, and dynamite.

"I hope you hit a richer lode than the Hidden Treasure," Pat said, referring to the biggest mine in the area, one that had produced millions of dollars and, until recently, employed over five hundred men. "This town's got a lot of life left in it. People like moving pictures, that's why I built the Starlight. Once Wisdom bounces back, it'll be packed every weekend."

Woody nodded worriedly to the distant town. "You oughtta check to make sure the whole joint ain't heading to Hades. That smoke's sure getting mighty heavy."

Pat grabbed up the binoculars. After a moment to focus in on his burning house, he breathed a sigh of relief. "It's just those buckets of tar I had left over from when I coated the roof of the theater. I had forgotten that I had stored them in the back bedroom. From what I can tell, Slow Ron's got everything wet down around the place and is waiting for the fire to burn itself out."

"Glad to hear the town's safe for a spell. I got an order to cut a couple of cords of wood for the Happy Eagle. Pearl and her girls will be needing it this winter. Sure won't be many miners about to keep them warm. I would venture that she oughtta rename her joint the Gloomy Eagle."

"I'll suggest it to her next time I get a chance."

"You keep spending time with Pearl Dunbar and that three grand will be a memory right shortly."

"She's not a bad sort. When I was in business back in Chicago during Prohibition, I had to deal with some gals that would make Pearl a shoe-in for sainthood."

"Still, I'll take my pay for that wood in cash instead of trade. I hear tell Carla's the only girl still working there and that she's about to starve out for lack of business."

Pat set the binoculars down and picked up his now empty glass. "I'm going to have another. Then maybe a double. I need to look plenty heartbroken when I drive into town and find my house has burned up. I wish I was a good actor like Errol Flynn or Edward G. Robinson, but I'm not. A few more jolts of scotch, however, and I can likely fool Slow Ron."

"He's the fire chief and marshal of a hick town that owns a gas station. He's also not smart enough to pour sand out of his shoes. It shouldn't take any Hollywood actor to fool that idiot. Arno Webster worked for him for five years before Ron finally figured out that every other dollar that went through his station went into Arno's pocket."

"Webster went to prison for that. He's been there since thirty-nine."

"Ah Pat, even a dolt can get lucky. I was just pointing out it took him five whole years to find out he was getting robbed blind. Slow Ron can count his fingers twice and come up with two different answers."

"Arson isn't a crime to be laughed at. If Slow Ron finds out what I just did and can prove it, I'll be up in Santa Fe sitting on a nail keg playing checkers with Arno Webster."

Woody studied on his answer while watching a bald eagle glide easily along on the rising air currents from the steep canyon below. "I suppose you oughtta have those drinks. Come to think on the matter, I'll be forced to join you. Scotch whiskey plays hob with my memory."

CHAPTER TWO

Alvin Kent pounded out the last bars of "Until the Real Thing Comes Along" on the worn ivories of the ancient upright piano. He then reached down, grabbed up his legs with both hands and swung himself around on the stool to where he could face Pearl Dunbar, whose approach he had seen in the mirror.

He hated the heavy steel leg braces and crutches he was forced to use because of a bout with polio when he was fourteen. Alvin was only twenty-three and wished desperately that he was able to join all of his friends in the war effort. It was an empty desire; he had difficultly moving his feet well enough to operate the pedals on the piano and keep his job as the professor for the Happy Eagle Bar.

Alvin received a meager ten dollars a month with room and board, along with an occasional tip from a drunken customer. Now that the town itself was dying around him, he wondered how long even this spare existence would last.

"That fire alarm this afternoon," Pearl said with a swish of her long red hair that sent a hint of spring roses past his nose, "was Pat Gunn's house. It burned completely to the ground. The poor man will be in a funk over losing everything so I want you to play something cheerful when he comes in."

The professor nodded knowingly. "How about I start with 'We're in the Money' and go from there?" Alvin's legs may have been crippled, but his mind worked just fine. He knew full well the rash of house fires that had been striking

Wisdom lately were not accidents.

"Well, keep the tunes happy. None of those tearjerkers. Folks have plenty to worry about these days without listening to sad piano music." The madam spoke with a pout on her ruby lips that Alvin had seen her wear whenever she was worried about something.

The lady he worked for was getting some years on her, but she was still beautiful. He guessed Pearl to be in her early forties. No one in town knew much about her, only that she had bought the place three years ago and was known for running the classiest brothel in this part of New Mexico. Pearl had piercing green eyes that complemented the curly red hair that cascaded to her trim waist like a waterfall of crimson flowers.

Alvin shot a furtive glance at the low-cut dress that showed without doubt Pearl Dunbar still had ample charms to turn any man's head, even his, if it was only possible. The polio had not affected his desires, but he believed no woman would ever go to bed with a cripple. Beside that, Pearl had, to the best of his knowledge, never gone to one of the back rooms with a man. The eight or ten young ladies she employed had kept the Happy Eagle plenty busy—until now.

"Bugger 'em. Bugger 'em good!" A shrill, grating voice whistled from inside of a large brass cage that hung from a chain at the far end of the long polished mahogany bar.

Pearl had come by the churlish macaw parrot shortly after her arrival in Wisdom. A British sailor had traded it to her for some services he badly wanted, but had no funds to pay for. Nero was the bird's name, given, it was said, because he was always fiddling with himself. Nero's screeching vocabulary was limited to British cuss words and off-color remarks. His propensity to bite, along with abrading nerves, caused the parrot to be universally hated by everyone except the madam, who doted on the colorful foul-beaked bird.

"Shut up, Nero, or I'll go catch an alley cat and put it in your cage," Carla Holland slurred from her seat at the bar.

"That would be one hell of a way to treat a perfectly good stray cat," Alvin said to the skinny girl with short dish-water blonde hair who was sipping on what was most likely her fifth drink, and darkness had yet to fully claim the day. "That parrot would shred a mountain lion's hiney. I shudder to think what he'd do to some innocent little house cat."

Pearl shook her head and turned to the cage. "Ah, poor Nero's all lonely," she cooed in a syrupy sweet voice. "Mommy's little dumpling just wants some attention."

"Hokey-pokey," Nero replied with a nerve-wracking screech. "Get a pokey."

"I wish some business would show up too, Nero," Carla said wistfully, turning her attention back to the whiskey and soda. It had been a long time since the amber fluid was able to buoy her sagging spirits, but it certainly beat facing reality without its help. "I haven't had a paying customer for two days now and I'm the only working girl in this hick town."

Pearl joined Alvin in casting a sad, anxious glance around the ornate parlor that was designed to pass for a fancy regular tavern to the unknowing eye. A lone nude picture of a reclining woman with decidedly ample charms behind the bottle-lined bar was the only outward sign of the delights that awaited any man who escorted a young lady through the red-curtained archway to one of the ten bedrooms that lined the rear of the building.

Aside from the rooms where the girls lived and worked, a

large kitchen and reading room gave a place of rest and refuge while assuring that none of them ever had to leave the bar and show their faces in public.

"Things have sure gotten dead hereabouts since the mines closed," Alvin commented. "The copper mines in Silver City are booming. Maybe someone will find copper here and things will get back to normal again."

Pearl's pout glided from her face easily as a white cloud on a sunny day when the chugging of an automobile engine could be heard out front. The car did not stop and continued on its way up the narrow canyon, gravel crunching under turning wheels.

"I thought for sure we had visitors," Alvin said. He moved himself around to face the piano again. "Business will pick up girls, don't you worry none."

"Can't get no worse," Carla said, chugging her drink.

"At least Pat should be by not too much later," Pearl said still staring out the front window.

The professor cracked his knuckles and began pounding out a tune that was popular a few years ago during the Great Depression, "You Can't Stop Me from Dreaming." There was no need to play anything happy until Pat showed up.

Then, he reflected, the madam would be smiling anyway. Alvin had become an astute observer of human behavior since polio had left him a cripple. Pearl Dunbar looked at Pat Gunn differently from all the other men who came into the Happy Eagle. The young man wondered how much more time would pass before the two of them saw in each other's eyes the same thing he did.

CHAPTER THREE

Pat Gunn was thoroughly and delightfully drunk, he decided, as he drove his 1932 Studebaker President Eight up the dry dirt road that ran past the cemetery to the remains of his house.

At least a couple of times on the way down from Woody's cabin he had found himself either driving on the wrong side of the highway or heading off it completely.

None of these were smart things to do on the narrow ribbon that wound snake-like over Angel's Roost Pass and dropped tortuously into the canyon town of Wisdom over a third of a mile below. Sheer drop-offs of over a hundred feet, unprotected by any form of guardrails, were common. People claimed that when the state of New Mexico had declared this road a state highway, the governor had laughed himself hoarse over the joke.

A smile had formed on his lips when he had driven past the sprawling two-story-high brick building proudly sporting the largest electrically lit sign in town that declared it to be the Starlight Theater.

Pat took pride in keeping the lights that flashed on and off in a circular fashion around the marquee on all day and all night, even though he had no films to show or, most importantly, there were very few people left in Wisdom to pay to come and see them. To him it was a way of fighting back against the oppressive dead calm that now covered the once-bustling town like a shroud.

Aside from the Starlight Theater, Joe and Irene Chapman's Bloated Goat Saloon two buildings west had an Open sign and lights on inside. Pat had noticed only two cars that he recognized as locals parked in front. The other business buildings, which stretched for blocks along what level ground was available in the narrow canyon and still leave room for Midas Creek and a road, were dark. Some were empty and boarded up, others had been simply abandoned with whatever wares that had been for sale still on the shelves. All were coffins of dreams.

A person had to make choices in this world, he reflected, as he made the final left turn before he would come to the smoking ruins of what had been his house.

Life demanded that the dice be tossed onto the green baize of chance. A person always lost whenever he or she became too afraid or confused to play the game. Those were the rules, like them or not. Pat Gunn had decided once again to roll the dice while betting on the value of gold, and with it, the future of the town of Wisdom.

Nine years ago he had made that very same decision when he had driven his then-new Studebaker into the remote but booming southwestern New Mexico town with ten thousand dollars cash in his pocket. At that time, Wisdom also had the additional lure of seeming to be the ideal place to start over and stay alive while doing so.

Pat Gunn had not always been the mild-mannered owner of a theater. A man did not come by a great deal of money during the Great Depression without at least bending a few rules. Pat had not only bent some rules, he had pummeled them.

His main reason for fleeing Chicago was Al Capone. He knew the famous gangster was now out of prison. He also had heard that Capone's body and mind were so destroyed by late-stage syphilis that he was forced to wear diapers and had to be led about like a pet dog. While this news was cheering, Al Capone was only one of the reasons Pat had chosen to stay single and seldom left town.

Pat Gunn had become immersed and totally enthralled with the make-believe world of movies. When he had first opened the Starlight Theater in June of 1933, the feature film was *Scarface*, starring Paul Muni. The irony had been delightful. Since that time he fondly remembered scores of wonderful movies that had played in his hundred-seat theater, which also sported a cozy balcony that could hold ten couples, most of whom were usually more interested in each other than watching whatever was flickering on the screen.

Mutiny on the Bounty, *Pennies from Heaven*, *Lost Horizon* and *The Grapes of Wrath*, all had played at the Starlight to a packed theater full of miners, along with their wives and children, who happily parted with a quarter during the evenings or fifteen cents for the Saturday matinee, to escape the dreariness of their existence.

And Pat Gunn had watched every minute of each one of the movies he showed, just as often as he could take his attention away from operating the projector. All movies were wonderful diversions into worlds a person could only dream of. The heroes were always men to look up to and know. Pat knew in his heart that, given the same situations, he would be just as stalwart and brave as Errol Flynn or Clark Gable. And the women were all so sensuous and tempting. Mae West and Joan Blondell were his favorite actresses to watch on the screen—or at least they had been until July. That was when he had been forced to stop showing his beloved movies.

It was then that the Hidden Treasure Mining Company had closed operations to comply with War Production

Board Ruling L-208. The government order was not to take effect until October, but to be patriotic the company had closed the mine early.

By August, the few young men in town with no ties had left. Since the Japanese had bombed Pearl Harbor last December, there were not a lot of young men working at the mine anyway. The outrage felt by the entire nation had caused most able-bodied men to quickly volunteer for service in the armed forces.

The government, in a furious drive to obtain raw materials for the war effort, had recognized this fact. To obtain manpower to extract desperately needed lead, copper, and zinc, the most expedient thing to do was make the mining of gold illegal for the duration. Men who were out of work would be forced to go to where there were jobs.

In September, the few smaller and outlying mines, such as the Mountain Lily, the Gold Dust and the Lucky Duck closed, throwing the last few dozen miners out of work. The exodus which had begun in July exhausted itself by the first of October and the small mountain town had reached its nadir.

Pat felt a wave of satisfaction when he thought of the three thousand dollars of insurance money he had coming and how that sum would surely tide him over until the war ended and things returned to normal. If he was frugal he could live on a hundred dollars a month.

The flashing red and blue lights atop the town's only police cruiser caught his full attention. It was parked in the middle of the narrow road in front of where his house had been. This came as no surprise and Pat took a quick, happy note that nothing but a concrete and stone foundation remained. Then he saw Ron Bowdrie drive a stake into the ground and tie a thin rope to it. This struck him as odd.

Pat pulled up behind the DeSoto and shut off his engine. He reminded himself that it was necessary to look totally distraught, painted a grimace on his face and staggered from his car.

Ron had likely been the fattest man in Wisdom before the great exodus. Nowadays, there was no contest. At well above three hundred pounds, Ron outweighed any competition by a large margin. The man gravitated toward politics like a duck takes to water. For years he had held the position of fire chief and town marshal, both of which he viewed as simply stepping stones to bigger and better things. He had no difficulty vividly picturing himself in the governor's mansion in Santa Fe. The fact that the town had become nearly deserted, along with the reality that he wouldn't be paid any longer because the town treasury was bankrupt, seemingly had yet to soak into his brain.

It was well known in Wisdom that what Ron Bowdrie hated worse than anything else was to be called Slow Ron. No one who cared to get along with him in the least ever called him that name anyplace except behind his back.

"Looks like Slow Ron has managed to save another foundation," Pat Gunn slurred, doing his best to look dismayed that his house had burned to the ground.

"You're going to lose that smart mouth of yours real soon, Gunn," Ron snarled.

Pat took a moment to sadly survey the ruins of his house. He then turned to the lawman who was the only person in the area beside himself.

"No reason to get nasty with me, Ron. My house has burned, along with everything in it. This is an awful thing to have happen."

"I'm sick to death of you people setting fire to your places for insurance money. When I'm finished with you, the state will have to take notice of what a great lawman I am."

"What are you getting at?" Pat was growing concerned and uncomfortably sober.

"I'm roping the area off," Ron retorted with obvious glee. "You and everyone else are ordered to stay out. Things are going to stay just as they are until I can get an arson investigator down from Santa Fe."

"Ron," Pat said, his voice muted with shock. "This was an accident. I spent the day helping Woody up at his place."

"If the investigator agrees it was an accident, which I sure as hell doubt, I'll take down the ropes and then you can claim your insurance money. Until that happens, I'll have to arrest you if you don't get your ass out of here and keep it out."

A suddenly sober Pat Gunn borrowed a line from Nero.

"Oh bugger," he said.

CHAPTER FOUR

Spinner Olsson flicked a silver dollar from between his thumb and forefinger, sending it twirling across the worn bar of the Bloated Goat Saloon. The gaunt white-haired, rheumy-eyed old fellow's lungs were so permeated with rock dust from too many years in the mines that he could only speak in short, wheezing sentences.

"Helluva world war we got ourselves into this time," Spinner gasped, retrieving his dollar for another twirl. The old man lived in a shack within easy walking distance of the saloon. For many years he had spent his days in the Bloated Goat sitting at the end of the bar drinking a nickel beer and spinning a silver dollar, which is how he had gotten his moniker. Since the attack on Pearl Harbor, a radio was kept on constantly, keeping patrons informed on news from the fronts.

"Those Nips sure caught Uncle Sam with his pants down, ain't no question about it," Fred Chapman said, extracting a bottle of beer from one of the two large white Frigidaires at the back of the room. He popped the top and resumed his seat on the stool behind the bar. "And there's submarines off the coast. It's just a matter of time until we'll be fighting that yellow horde right here on our own soil."

"We just got in some of those blue light bulbs to use to blackout the joint if they start bombing us here," Irene, Fred's wife of forty-nine years said after finishing her mint julep. "There's enough problems in Wisdom without helping those Japs add to our pain."

"She's gotten real upset about sugar being rationed," Fred said to Spinner with a nod. "Even powdered sugar's included, so Irene's plenty worried about being able to keep making her mint juleps. I keep trying to tell her that Wisdom ain't gonna be bombed."

"Everything you read is always telling folks to grow a victory garden," Irene said testily. "Mint and rhubarb's the only things that'll grow up here and not get frostbit to death in July. I'm growing mint and doing my part for the war effort. Rhubarb pie takes one heck of a lot more sugar than a little julep on occasion."

"It's just that Irene comes up with lots of occasions every day," Fred said with an evil grin. "I reckon that's all right, keeps her happy."

"Being happy these days is a stretch," Lonnie Dillman said from down the bar. The only paying customer in the Bloated Goat wore grease-soaked overalls that hadn't been changed during the three weeks he had been in town busting up any scrap iron he could find and trucking it off to Silver City. "I sure hope they make a big bomb out of the scrap I haul in, and drop it square on Hitler's noggin."

"That would be nice." Spinner gasped. "The sooner the war's over, the sooner this town'll get back to booming again."

"This war's gonna last a long spell," Lonnie said. "My guess is this place will die before it's over. Hell's bells, I'm hauling off most of the mining machinery in these parts for scrap iron and splitting the money with the mine owners. Those folks sure don't have a lot of faith in things getting better right shortly and I can't blame them for not wanting to pay property tax on a bunch of stuff just sitting there rusting away."

"Those are only the little mines that you're scrapping out," Fred said firmly before taking a swig of beer. "The Hidden Treasure's ready to run again anytime."

"I wrote Ira Tischler, the president of that company back in New York. He answered me, saying they were going to hold a board meeting soon and would consider my offer to scrap out both the mine and mill. He added that they were going to do what they felt would best aid in the war effort." Lonnie signed. "If the Axis wins this war, there ain't nothing much that'll matter then."

"We're gonna win," Spinner wheezed. "An' folks are gonna need something to come back to."

"That's right," Irene said using both hands on the counter to help her stand. She was slender as a willow tree, but rheumatism and old age caused her to walk stooped and use a cane. "There's millions of dollars worth of gold in these hills. Folks will always be mining hereabouts. Fred an' me will still be here to sell them drinks."

"I surely hope you're right, Ma'am," Lonnie said. "I plain admire the way you people are hanging on. That motion picture theater keeps its lights on all the time. I notice they aren't showing any movies, but it makes the place look optimistic, just the same."

"Pat Gunn came here in thirty-two and built the Starlight. He used to come in here a lot, but lately he's taken to drinking at the Happy Eagle," Fred said. "Pat's gonna stay here for sure."

"The madam there's a slick chick." Spinner gave his silver dollar another twirl. "I don't blame him for having the hots. There used to be girls working all up and down that canyon." He took a moment to catch his breath. "I hear tell there's only a couple left."

"There was just one whore there last week," Lonnie said

as he slid his empty beer glass toward Fred. "A mousy blonde, but she wouldn't go back to the room with me unless I took a bath. If there's anything I can't abide, it's a finicky woman."

Fred stood and went to take another bottle of beer from the cooler. "Females do have a tendency to get uppity." He wagged his head at Irene. "Especially when they've been hanging around for a lot of years. I'll have to say she's the oldest woman I ever went to bed with."

"Keep quiet you old poop," Irene shuffled by her husband. "Or you'll wind up sleeping on the couch. I'm heading out by the creek and pick some more mint. I suffered enough through Prohibition. Sugar rationing or not, I'm going to make myself another mint julep."

Fred opened the beer, set it down in front of Lonnie and rang up fifteen cents on the big brass cash register before returning to his stool. He turned to the slamming of the screen door. "I hope that woman didn't go and let any skeeters in. That's the only good thing about winter up here, no skeeters to put up with."

Spinner turned his attention to his old friend, Fred. "I hear Slow Ron's on the prod about houses burning. That idiot wants a cushy job with the state something fierce. We'll be better off when he loads up that wife of his and leaves."

"Ron's a bad apple. Why Minnie puts up with him is a mystery. That poor woman never comes to town unless she's sporting a nasty bruise someplace or has an arm in a sling."

"He never beats on her before any election dinner or when some government fellow's coming to visit," Spinner added.

Fred clucked his tongue and ran bony fingers through

his short silver hair. "Pat Gunn's place up on the hill burnt to the ground this afternoon. I hope Ron don't go and give him any grief."

Lonnie spoke up, "I heard the fire alarm, then noticed the smoke. I saw a house was what was burning. The Mountain Lily's where I'm scrapping. A person can look right down on the town from there. This Ron fellow, he's the law hereabouts I reckon. A mighty fat fellow by that name came waddling up where I was working a few days ago. He flashed a badge and asked me my business. I showed him a copy of an agreement I had with the owners. That man looked mighty disappointed when he couldn't arrest me."

"That's our Slow Ron alright." Fred sighed. "He owns the gas station on the right as you come into town. Ron's been plaguing Wisdom as marshal and fire chief for years."

"Why, I've bought gasoline for my truck there at that station. A mighty nice looking lady with short brown hair waited on me. Come to think on the matter, she did have one arm badly bruised up. I noticed that when her sleeve slid down her arm when she reached up on a shelf to get a quart of oil. I can't feature a cute tomato like her sticking with a fat slob who beats on her."

Spinner took a rattling breath and wheezed. "A woman's something a man can't figger. He'll just burn out his thinker trying."

"Still," Lonnie grumbled, "badge or not, it ain't right to go and pound on some little gal for any reason."

"It wouldn't work with Irene," Fred said firmly. "That woman would pound back."

"I heard that you old poop," Irene said, coming back in with one hand full of mint while brushing off a few huge flakes of snow from her gray hair with the other. "Ron

Bowdrie's lazy and worthless as well as being despicable and meaner than a rattlesnake with boils. The people up in Santa Fe know that. They're not as dumb as Ron thinks they are. Being a lawman in Wisdom is as far up the government ladder that fool will ever climb."

"From the looks of things," Lonnie said with a flick of his hand toward the front window, "there's not much need of law here these days."

"And even less money to pay for it," Fred interjected. "Slow Ron's going to have to either take over running the gas station and try to make it pay or leave town and make a living for a spell—"

A flash of blue light lit the street in front of the saloon. Seconds later a roaring boom rattled the racks of bottles and glasses behind the bar.

"Lightning and thunder while it's spitting snow," Irene said. "I haven't seen the likes of that up here before."

Lonnie took a gulp of beer. "When I was just a kid, my grandpappy told me that means the Devil was coming to town pushing a wood cart to carry away your soul in."

"The Devil's going to come up empty-handed in Wisdom," Spinner Olsson gasped, but his worried expression showed that he was not convinced.

CHAPTER FIVE

Pat Gunn was jolted awake by what he thought was a distant rifle shot. This was the first night he had spent in the small apartment he had built in the long, narrow room behind the screen of his theater. Being in strange surroundings, it took him a moment to get his mind in order. A throbbing headache from too much whiskey wasn't helping.

He climbed out of the small cot and quickly wrapped up in a thick quilt robe. The room was cold as the inside of an icebox. He had neglected to build a fire when he came home from the Happy Eagle last night. Another distant explosion brought him to look out one of two windows in his room.

A light skiff of snow blanketed the empty streets. It was obvious that not a single vehicle had gone by to mar the perfect whiteness, even though the clock on the wall showed it to be nearly nine in the morning.

When a third blast thudded across the stillness of the valley, it dawned on Pat what the ruckus was. That scrapper from Sliver City was using mudcapping to blow cast iron into pieces small enough to be loaded on a truck by hand. Dynamite cartridges were slit open and the filler laid on the piece of machinery to be demolished. Once a blasting cap and fuse had been laid out properly, a thick covering of mud was placed over the explosive, which directed the charge inward with shattering force.

Most likely the scrapper was blowing up the huge air compressor at the Mountain Lily Mine. Pat had seen it years earlier when Woody and he had visited the long inactive part of the mine high on the mountain. Installed late in the 1890s, the monstrous machine sported two flywheels that must have been ten feet in diameter and weigh into the tons. At the time he had marveled over the elegant machine and as to how something of such monstrous weight had been transported to a remote site like the Mountain Lily Mine long before there were trucks and bulldozers.

Now, a few loads of scrap iron to feed the war effort would be the legacy of another piece of antique machinery. There were not many mines left to scrap, he mused, but when gold came back the miners would surely bring in modern diesel or electric machinery to work with. There was no need to concern himself over some old junk iron being blown apart and hauled away.

He flicked on the hot plate that sat on a counter next to the window to warm, while he went to check out the coal-burning potbelly Ajax stove. The coal scuttle was empty and he had neglected to bring in any kindling wood.

"Damn weather up here," he swore to himself. "One day it's hot enough to fry an egg on the roof, the next you've got icicles hanging off your ass."

Pat plugged an electric heater into an outlet and hunkered over it as thin metal coils wound around a porcelain cylinder began glowing a cheery red. It was a heater just like this one that he had left on in his house yesterday. A pile of dirty, worn-out clothes heaped close in front of it, along with a few kerosene lamps atop a nearby dresser, had done exactly what he had hoped.

All he had wanted was enough money to hang on for a while. It was not like he had robbed a bank or hurt anyone. Insurance companies were all crooks and despots that made Hitler look like a choirboy by comparison. They were loaded with cash and he was broke. He considered that a fair incentive to get back some of the premium money he had paid over the years.

Then Slow Ron, for the first time in all of the years he had known the lazy slob, had thrown a monkey wrench into the works by acting like a real lawman.

Warmer now, Pat filled a small pan with cold water from the sink and set it on the hotplate. Into a heavy mug he spooned a generous amount of G. Washington's instant coffee. One of the good things to come along with modern times was the fact that a man suffering with a hangover didn't have to wait until a pot of coffee perked to get some badly needed relief.

Pat could not help but worry about the arson investigator Ron had threatened to bring in. He had taken more pains than most to make his house fire appear to be an accident. Up until now, most folks had simply dashed some gasoline about, tossed matches over their shoulders on the way out, then driven to Silver City to pick up their checks.

No, there's nothing on that hill for any investigator to find even if they sift through every ounce of ashes, Pat thought. *It was just an accidental electrical fire that needed some encouragement. I can't get sent to prison without solid evidence.*

But Ron Bowdrie's actions certainly could delay him getting his check from the insurance company for an awfully long while. A grimace crossed Pat's face like a black cloud when he remembered that he had less than two hundred dollars to his name.

He went back and hunkered over the heater while taking a mental inventory. He had laid in sacks of cornmeal, flour and pinto beans. There were ample stocks of sugar, salt and canned items such as jalapeño peppers that he loved to eat with peanut butter.

No, he wouldn't go hungry. The Studebaker could stay parked most of the time and save burning expensive gasoline that was now up to an unbelievable eighteen cents a gallon. The electric and water bills were averaging twenty dollars a month for both. He nodded with satisfaction that he would be all right for a while. Back when the theater was still operating, he had laid in twelve tons of coal to fire the big boiler in the basement. That much coal being used in his small potbelly stove would last the winter and most of the next.

Pat decided he could also work, if it came to a disaster. Woody chopped firewood for his money these days. There was no reason he couldn't do the same. He was in solid shape for forty-nine years of age. There might be silver streaking his black hair and a crick in his back on occasion, but the paunch around his middle would quickly disappear with a little hard work like chopping firewood.

It was Pearl Dunbar that concerned him the most. He sincerely enjoyed the madam's company and had been spending every night at her place. He had never paid one of the girls who worked there for a romp in a back room. Nor had he ever asked Pearl to go to bed with him.

There was just something about the sweet smelling redhead that attracted him with a lure that surpassed sensuality. There was nothing about their relationship he could explain. Pearl had most likely been a whore, even though she never spoke of it.

Then again, he realized, Pat Gunn was no saint himself. Not by a *very* long shot.

Pearl charged him a quarter for every drink he had there. Four drinks a night only totaled up to thirty dollars a month. Chicken feed to a business owner. Spending time with that lovely lady was worth every dime.

He made a note to ask Woody how much a cord of firewood sold for, then went and poured boiling water into his coffee cup. There was no reason to get into a funk over Slow Ron's antics. An old adage said that all good things come to them who wait.

Pat Gunn sipped his black coffee and wondered deeply if the old philosopher who had said that knew fly shit from pepper.

CHAPTER SIX

The sun died early in Wisdom. The jagged spires of Angel's Roost Mountain in the west reached heavenward with a craggy hand to blot out the warming rays of that orange orb and replace its cheeriness with enshrouding shadows.

This day it was as if the departing sun had dragged a heavy and frigid layer of cold over the remote town and left it hanging in its wake like an icy breath from the Grim Reaper.

Around midday the ever-present wind had shifted directions to drive away the gray storm clouds and allow the sun's brief appearance time to turn what snow had accumulated into water. The bitter cold of night had painted the streets and walkways with a treacherous covering of ice. Winter had come hard to Wisdom.

"Any brass monkeys left outside tonight will sure as hell be singing soprano tomorrow," Link Dawson said, batting his hands against the sleeves of his coat as Joe Godfrey and he came inside the Happy Eagle Bar.

"Hello there boys, good to have you drop by," Pearl Dunbar said with a sincere smile, coming to help the men out of their coats. "A good stiff drink's what a man needs to keep his circulation in order when it's cold out."

"Whiskey an' a poke," Nero squawked loud enough to drown out Alvin's piano playing. "Bugger like a bunny. Drink like a fish."

Joe Godfrey cocked an eye at the parrot. "That's one dirty mouthed bird you've got there, Pearl."

"Oh, not really," the madam said soothingly. "Nero only says what most men are thinking. He's just not bothered by a lot of conscience."

"Thanksgiving is coming," Carla Holland said sitting alone at a table. "The professor and me are planning to cook up that parrot instead of a turkey. The dinner won't be much, but the party afterward will make up for any shortcomings."

Carla leaned back to show off her small firm breasts. She ran her tongue over her lips to moisten them and smiled hopefully at the two men. There was little chance old man Godfrey would ask her to go to a room. He owned the restaurant and bakery in town. Not only was he married, the fellow was old enough that the lead had likely gone out of his pencil. Link was another story altogether. He was younger and owned a large ranch a few miles from town. He had taken girls to a back room here plenty of times. The rancher was surely married but so were most of her customers. What concerned her was the fact that he liked his girls very young. Something she no longer was.

"Buy me a drink, boys?" Carla asked with a silken voice.

Link snorted, shook his head, and said to Pearl as Joe and he headed for the bar. "When are you going to get in some pretty ones? Money's too tight these days to blow on a skinny old whore."

Carla kept her practiced smile and turned her attention back to the whiskey sour. Link Dawson's words had stung like hornets, yet she could not show it. What hurt most of all was the fact that the man hadn't even acknowledged her existence. Carla would only be thirty-three her next birthday, but she knew that in her profession she was already old and used up. What ripped her soul worse than any words ever could was the stark realization that she had no other place to go, or anyone to go to. She took a hefty swallow of whiskey and silently prayed for its amber currents to carry away her troubles.

"I've got some calls out," Pearl said cheerfully. She went behind the bar. "Name your poison, gents." The madam held hope that, as sometimes happened, a few drinks might plaster a lot of beauty on a rather plain-looking working girl. If Carla took off, she would have to close the place or go back to doing what she used to. There was surely no reason for any new girls to come to Wisdom.

"Howdy, Joe—Link," Pat Gunn said cheerfully from his usual seat at the most distant bar stool from Nero. "Colder than an Eskimo's nose out there, isn't it?"

"Give us both a bottle of beer," Link said plunking down a fifty-cent piece on the bar. He turned to Pat. "I reckon congratulations on your house burning down would be in order, but Joe here filled me in about Slow Ron trying to act like a real lawman for a change. Tough break he had to wait and try to improve himself on you."

"Things will work out," Pat said with a shrug. "I was up at Woody's all that afternoon. My house plain went and caught fire all by its lonesome. Woody's out alongside the bar unloading firewood from his Model A. When he comes in, you can ask him yourself."

"Ain't me that needs convincing." Link took a swig of beer. "It'll likely be that investigator from Santa Fe. Hell, I'd expect you done a good enough job not to fret. Much anyway."

"Ron Bowdrie's plenty afraid of having to get a real job," Joe said. "He claimed that the Army turned him down because he was needed here. My guess is he didn't even try to join. He's too fat and lazy, aside of being scared to death of being shot at. That wife of his does all the work at the gas station. All Ron does is set in the firehouse all day long playing solitaire. If he can't get a cushy government job in Santa Fe, he'll be doomed to actual work, so I venture he's mighty desperate to make a good showing."

Pat Gunn smiled and tinkled hailstones around in his glass of scotch. Pearl, along with Woody, kept a supply on hand for him in the freezing compartment. "I'm not going to get into a funk over the matter. The way I see it, anybody they send down here from Santa Fe will have to be smarter than Slow Ron. They'll figure out plenty fast I suffered a pure accident."

"Here's to getting money from insurance companies," Joe said holding up his beer. "Maude an' me would've been forced to close our place long before now if it wasn't for them."

"What do you mean, before now?" Pat asked, raising an eyebrow.

"We're finished come tomorrow. There ain't no way or reason to hang on. Between the electric, water, and supplies, Maude and me are losing twelve dollars a week just keeping the doors open for folks who never come by."

"Wisdom will boom again, soon," Pat said firmly. "I read an article in the paper that said the war will be over in a month or two. The government's got some new secret weapon."

"If it's a secret," Link asked, "how did they come to write about it?"

"How am I supposed to know? It *has* to be the truth because it was right there in black and white."

The slamming of the front door took everyone's attention.

"Dang-nab it, Pearl," Woody said loudly. "From the woolly-booger this winter's shaping up to be you oughtta buy a couple more cords of wood for sure. I'm laying in a big supply of smoking tobacco. Can't afford to take any chance with my health at my age."

Pearl bent over and began fishing for money from her purse that she kept on a shelf under the bar. The men grew silent as they gazed upon ample and tempting cleavage that strained mightily against a tight-fitting low-cut green dress.

She stood and laid out a five-dollar bill along with an equal number of singles on the mahogany counter as Woody approached, wearing a big smile.

"I'll have to make do with the one cord for awhile," Pearl said before Woody could ask again. "There's a fair supply of coal in the bin."

"Just give me a holler and I'll bring you some more before you can say Jack Robinson," Woody grabbed up his money, peeled off a dollar bill and tucked the balance into a pocket of his khaki shirt. "Give me a beer and—" He hesitated a moment before nodding toward Carla, "one of whatever the little lady's having. She looks terrible lonesome sitting there by herself."

Seldom did anything take Pearl aback, but this turn of events succeeded. She whisked the look of amazement from her face by quickly beginning to make a whiskey sour while wondering what the old miner was planning. He had never spent more than thirty cents in her bar before and certainly had never given any of the girls more than a passing glance.

Alvin, always one to keep an eye on proceedings in the Happy Eagle, began stroking the ivories to an old hit tune that seemed appropriate to the occasion, "I'm in the Mood for Love."

Woody picked up his sixty cents in change, mildly surprised that a whiskey sour cost the same as a simple shot of scotch dumped over God's free hailstones. He pocketed the money, grabbed up the drinks and strode over to Carla's table. "Could I join you, Ma'am?"

"I would like that mister—Woody, isn't it?" Carla noticed a tone of sincerity in her voice that sounded so strange it was as if someone else was speaking.

"That's what my daddy called me nigh onto sixty years ago. I've been going by it ever since. The last name's always been Johnson, too."

"Carla Holland's mine," she beamed as Woody sat down and scooted the whiskey sour toward her. "Most working girls always use another name, but I never have. There's no family out there for me to embarrass. I was only eight when the Spanish flu took my parents. All of my other relatives need the shock, if they ever found out."

"Sorry to hear about what happened to your folks, miss."

"It's Carla. Please call me that."

"Carla it is, Ma'am. I've been hacking away at a mine up on Angel's Roost Mountain since nineteen-fifteen. It's supposed to be a gold mine, but so far it's too early to say for certain."

"Thanks for the drink, Woody." She batted her dark eyelashes and motioned with a nod toward the red curtain. "Would you like to get to know me a *lot* better?"

"Yes Ma'am, ah—Carla, I surely expect that would be a pleasure. But I'm fond of my victuals and I can buy a lot of bacon and pancake flour, not to mention cigarette tobacco, for what a fling on the mattress would run me."

"That's all right," she said quickly with a note of desperation. "Pearl would toss me out on my ear if I didn't at least ask. Could you please just stay and visit? I promise I won't be a bother."

Woody grinned and nodded. He had not talked with a

pretty girl for so long he felt as if he were young again.

A wracking cough accompanied the opening of the front door. All eyes turned to watch the wheezing Spinner Olsson as he shuffled his way to the bar, leaning heavily on a cane.

Pearl waited patiently until the old fellow had managed to climb onto a stool and caught as much breath as he was able. "What can I get you, sir?"

"How much for a glass of beer, the cheap kind? A short one's a nickel at the Goat."

The madam clucked her tongue and gave the patrons a furtive glance. She didn't buy beer by the keg. Bottled beer sold for fifteen cents with a good profit. It would set a dangerous precedent to charge one customer less than the others and do so in plain sight. Then a thought struck. She went to the refrigerator, took out a bottle of beer and popped the top on the opener at the end of the bar. A regular-sized drink glass held about a third of the beer, allowing for a goodly head.

"A short beer costs the same here, too," Pearl said proudly.

Spinner cast a jaundiced eye at the glass that was considerable smaller than those Fred used at the Bloated Goat. Then his gaze settled on Pearl's well-exposed bosom. "Fair enough, Ma'am. Reckon I might take to spending some time here. Leastwise I will when the weather's better. I slipped on the ice a couple of times heading up here. Dang near slid all the way into Midas Creek, but I managed to catch hold of a tree branch."

"I'll drive you back home in my car," Pat Gunn said. He was continually complaining about the cost of gasoline and the growing scarcity of tires, yet no one in Wisdom had ever caught him walking over a block from wherever he called home. His black Studebaker, the rear tires wrapped with snow chains, sat in front of the bar. Less than two blocks down the canyon the flashing lights from the marquee of the Starlight Theater were plainly visible against the darkness.

"What brought you out on a night slippery enough to nearly give you a cold bath in the creek," Joe Godfrey asked. "Did the Chapmans go and close down the Bloated Goat?"

Spinner made two gasps and took a long swallow of beer before he had built up enough wind to answer. "No, the Goat's gonna stay open. Irene's passed out at the bar snoring like a buzz saw with a chipped tooth. Fred's listening to Glen Miller on the radio." He wheezed with a deep rattle that sounded more like a gurgle, then continued, "No one there to talk to after Slow Ron went home."

Pat raised an eyebrow. "Did Ron have anything intelligent to say or was he having a usual night?"

"That's one reason I decided to brave the ice. I thought you ought to know he's going to Silver City in the morning and bring back that investigator from Santa Fe. They'll be here in town before dark."

"I thought that feller would drive down from the capital," Link said.

"The state's cutting back on gas. Ron's going to pick him up at the bus depot. Keller's the lawman's name, Frank Keller."

"If he's good at his job, I'll have my insurance check in a few days," Pat said hopefully.

"You'd better just hope like hell he ain't *too* good," Spinner said.

"I don't know what it would feel like to live in a real home and be able to stay in one spot for years," Carla said to the genial old miner. "I've worked mining camps from Arizona to Montana. Most places what I did was against the law. Everything I own will fit into a suitcase. I haven't always had a lot of time to plan ahead as to when I'd be leaving town."

Woody finished the final swig of beer from his bottle and asked Pearl to bring them another. He had noticed Spinner hobble in but paid scant attention to what anyone at the bar had to say. He could talk to other men any time he pleased.

"Your perfume smells like spring cherry blossoms," Woody said. "I really like it."

Carla smiled sweetly.

Woody leaned back and stared off into space, worrying his stubby white beard with one hand. "I envy you seeing other places. That cabin of mine gets plenty stale. It's just that I've got a rich vein doodlebugged out. I use a brass rod with a bottle of mercury and a little piece of gold taped to one end. Those things never fail to locate ore. The problem is, with so blasted many veins in the area, the doodlebug gets sort of confused. Mine's been trying to sort out Angel's Roost Mountain for twenty-seven years."

"You'll find gold. I feel it in my bones. You're one lucky man, Woody Johnson."

Pearl brought over their drinks. Woody paid for them then leaned his elbows on the table and gazed wordlessly at the slender girl. He honestly believed that Carla was the most beautiful woman in the world. He also wondered deeply if perhaps there might be other kinds of gold than the cold, yellow variety he had pursued all those many years.

CHAPTER SEVEN

Pat Gunn placed a fist to his chin and studied the flashing lights of the marquee with a wrinkled brow. At least a dozen bulbs had burned out and required changing, not one of his favorite tasks. He got distinctly nervous whenever his feet were on a wobbly ladder, a long distance above terra firma. At least he remembered it being that way. It had been years since he had actually been on a ladder.

He sighed when he thought back to when he had money to hire some kid to do these kinds of jobs. Keeping the lights on was actually an act of absurdity, he realized, but it was something he felt compelled to do. The town of Wisdom was not dying, it was simply taking a prolonged intermission.

After several minutes he resigned himself to the likelihood that no one would drop by who he could cajole into climbing a ladder. With a shrug he began heading for the storage shed alongside the theater to drag out the long wobbly wood ladder and grab up some new light bulbs.

One consolation was the improvement in the weather. It was approaching high noon and this day had become an antithesis of yesterday. The temperature felt to be in the seventies and a cheerful sun beamed down from a cloudless azure sky. On the downside, the warm weather had also brought to life hoards of mosquitoes and gnats, along with a particularly irritating species of large green fly that seemed best adept at dying by droves. Early this morning one fly had crashed into his bowl of oatmeal while hundreds of his companions kept buzzing against the windows until dropping dead and falling onto the sills in long, dark rows.

"Delightful climate up here," Pat mumbled, slapping at whatever had decided to crawl into his ear. "I simply can't imagine living anywhere else."

Once he had the ladder in place, resting high on the marquee, Pat found that changing the light bulbs was not as bad as he had feared. The first thing he had learned was to never look down. By concentrating on the job at hand, all fifteen burned-out bulbs had been replaced in minutes.

He climbed down, tossed the bad bulbs from the gunnysack he had draped around his neck into a trash can, then studied his workmanship.

While all of the light bulbs now flashed merrily around the edge of the marquee, the large area where the letters were meant to be placed to announce the feature films, along with the names of the stars, was depressingly white and blank. This was a problem that could easily be remedied, especially now that he realized he could actually climb a ladder without suffering a disaster.

The large square of plywood with pockets for all letters of the alphabet was imposing at first, but determination drove him now. Pat scurried skyward and hung the letter board on one of the metal pegs set into the sign for that purpose. He then began sorting capital letters from the lower case, all the while wondering deeply what title to advertise.

The words COMING ATTRACTION did not require a lot of thought. He knew full well that it might be some time before he could actually afford to rent a film to show, but his friends and neighbors in Wisdom needed cheering. A light, funny movie to look forward to would be the ticket.

Then he remembered a movie he had gotten posters for that seemed absolutely perfect. After several minutes of stretching to align letters, Pat climbed down, backed off, took time to light up a Camel cigarette, then studied his handiwork.

NEVER GIVE A SUKER AN EVEN BREAK STARRING W. C. FIELDS, looked back at him like a promise from God.

The movie, if he remembered correctly, would cost him a minimum of seven dollars for a short run, which was two days. The pesky arithmetic involved in what the motion picture industry termed "gate receipts" could certainly be avoided in Wisdom, New Mexico for the foreseeable future.

Almost before he realized it, Pat was adding up just how many of the people still hanging on here might part with a quarter to see a movie. His mental cash register stopped whirling at one dollar. Still, he decided to give the matter some more thought. Perhaps he could place an ad in the Silver City newspaper. This might bring in enough ranchers who lived nearby, along with a few good folks who like to drive out of town for—

Damn it all, tires are rationed and getting scarce as hen's teeth. Gasoline is expensive and often hard to find. Until this war is over, I'm only dreaming.

Feeling dejected now, he replaced the ladder, along with the letter box, back into the shed. He was closing the door when he saw Spinner Olsson shuffling by on his cane. He decided to walk over and visit for a bit. There was certainly nothing else more important pressing his time. It would be several hours before he could head for the Happy Eagle and not run out of money before time to go to bed.

"Thanks for the lift last night," Spinner said. "Who'd look about now and believe there was ice all over the joint then?"

"I'd felt plumb guilty if you'd slid into the creek. For

miles downstream those poor trout would've been green about the gills, not to mention the fact that they wouldn't be edible for years."

Spinner ignored the gibe and studied the marquee. "When is this coming attraction actually coming?"

"Just as soon as the war's over and I can afford to bring it to town."

The old man wheezed to catch his breath. "That being the case, I'd reckon most everybody will be looking plenty forward to seeing that movie."

"It won't be a lot longer."

"At my age, I'm only planning on making it up to Pearl's joint. I'm going to start spending my nickels there, leastwise I am when it ain't too slick to walk that far. The Goat's closer but there's never anyone to visit with there these days. Irene passes out early and Fred had rather listen to the radio than talk. Besides, Pearl's got a great pair of *maracas*. Takes me back to when I was young."

Pat cocked his head. "As old as you are, I'm surprised you remember what those are."

"Can't do nothing about 'em anymore, but I sure do like to look. Ain't no harm in that. A man has to get out once in awhile and see the sights. Aside of that, when it's real bad weather out, I'll read a good book." Spinner rolled his eyes to the sign on the marquee. "You don't much fancy books, do you Pat?"

Pat shrugged. "My business keeps me way too busy to read, has for years."

Spinner shifted his gaze up and down the lifeless streets. "I reckon it does at that."

The old man stuck his cane out to continue his slow walk down the canyon when the distant chugging of an engine caught both his attention and Pat's.

After a moment, a wood-body Ford Model C station wagon turned onto Main Street from the road that led to the cemetery beyond where Pat's burned-out house had stood. The men recognized the battered car as belonging to an older couple who lived in a small frame home past the road fork on the outskirts of town.

"That's the Jenkins' coming, isn't it?" Pat asked.

"Nope, those are the Jordans, Oliver and Harriet; they've lived up there for maybe thirty years, longer than I've been in these parts."

"They never get out much."

"If folks don't go to the movies," Spinner coughed long and hard before he could catch his breath and continue, "or spend time in a cathouse or bar, you'd be apt not to know 'em."

"Just seen them around is all."

"Oliver used to work at the Hidden Treasure, same as me. He was smart enough to work in the mill rather than the mine. He's lucky enough to be retired on Social Security and be able to breathe."

The duo watched as the considerably battered old station wagon rumbled by, its four-cylinder engine chugging hard against the grade. Both Pat and Spinner waved, only to be ignored by the white-haired old couple who sat bent over in the front seat, staring ahead as if they were frozen into position.

"That beats all," Spinner said. "I can understand 'em giving you the cold shoulder, but Oliver and me's been friends for a long while."

"Perhaps they've got things on their mind."

Spinner watched as the car disappeared up the narrow ribbon of road and into the pine trees, heading for Silver

City. "Yeah, I'd reckon that's all it amounts to." He gave out a gurgling wheeze, then once again started his trek. "I'll warn Pearl you're coming by later," he said over his shoulder. A few moments later he was gone.

The shadows of late afternoon found Lonnie Dillman and Woody Johnson poking through Woody's extensive collection of worn-out, rusty machinery that littered the area around his Angel Roost Mine.

"That rock crusher was likely last used by Noah to crush up ballast for the bottom of the ark," Lonnie said with a cluck of his tongue as he inspected the last piece of machinery that Woody had said he would part with.

Woody snorted. "You're gonna smash it up and haul it into Silver City to be sent off to a steel mill. There's no call to insult it, too."

Dillman grinned through the black smears of grease that covered his face. He was beginning to like the old prospector. "Right now, scrap metal's worth more than gold mines. I'll have to say that you're hauled a lot of iron in here over the years."

Woody lowered an eyebrow and decided he would be smart not to elaborate on exactly how he had come by most of it. A closed mine, with no one packing a gun watching the place, certainly meant it was abandoned. However, this was a philosophy that many narrow-minded lawmen would probably not agree with. But, he reminded himself, possession *was* nine-tenths of the law.

"How much do you think I can get out the stuff I showed you?" Woody asked hopefully.

Lonnie's face tightened in concentration. "Well, the final tally will be decided by the scales down in Silver. I'll show you the tickets when we settle up. Like I told you, I keep half of all the money for busting it up and trucking it." He glared at Woody.

"Yep, that's my understanding, too."

"Well, sir, my best guess is there's a solid hundred and fifty tons of good scrap here. Possibly more. I'd be safe in saying that the least you'll get, if we make a deal, would be over two hundred dollars."

Woody swallowed hard. That was more money than he had ever had in one spot his entire life. "Then I reckon we've got that deal."

Lonnie extended a hand, which was eagerly grasped by the old prospector. "I'll get started day after tomorrow. I'll be finished with the Mountain Lily by then."

"Sooner the better."

"If you're in bad straits . . ." Lonnie hesitated. Conversations like these often got him into trouble. "Like if you're hungry or something, I'll advance you a couple of dollars."

"That's okay, sonny boy," Woody said as he watched relief cross the scrapper's smeared face. "I can wait. It's just that I've begun making different plans. I'm keeping the Smith air compressor and what few things up here that actually work. I'll keep plugging away at mining, but sometimes a man starts thinking different."

Lonnie grinned evilly. "At least you're too old to be doing your thinking below your belt buckle like a lot of men do."

Woody gave Dillman an expression usually reserved for folks being carted off to an insane asylum, took out the fixings and began to roll a cigarette. He had just moistened the paper when, in the stone quiet of the mountains, near where the road made one of its many sharp bends, a rifle shot cracked.

"Someone's out hunting a deer," Lonnie said, turning to

face in the direction the sound had come from.

"Could be."

There was a definite squealing of tires, followed by the harsh sound of crashing metal and breaking glass.

"That's a car wreck for certain," Lonnie shouted. "Hop in my truck and we'll go see what we can do to help."

The Angel Roost Mine was only about a quarter of a mile from the main road. When Lonnie pulled onto the blacktop, the car they had heard crash was now sending up spires of flame and black smoke. The DeSoto's front end was wrapped around a sturdy pine tree, its rear tires still on the blacktop.

"That's the cop car!" Lonnie blurted.

"And there's Slow Ron climbing out of the driver's side. I'm surprised the idiot ever made it once over this road without running off it. Looks like his dumb luck finally run out on him."

Lonnie slammed on the brakes, bringing his large truck to a screeching halt scant feet away from the smoking police cruiser.

"Looky there, in the passenger seat. That's a man slumped over the dash. We gotta help him."

Lonnie Dillman's words had not cleared the air when the mountainside in front of them exploded into a huge orange ball of billowing flames.

CHAPTER EIGHT

"Oh my God," Woody exclaimed as he flung open the door and jumped out. "That man still in the car has to be the investigator Ron went to pick up."

"Grab a fire extinguisher," Lonnie yelled. "There's a big brass one in the toolbox under the truck bed. I'll get the one on my side. We've got to get those flames out now!"

Lonnie aimed the stream from his Pyrene Extinguisher at the source of the inferno. Woody, on the other hand, was spraying the liquid straight into the flames. That was not the way to put out a fire. Before he could say anything, both extinguishers sputtered their last gasp.

Woody studied the situation as he skirted the lowering flames on his way over to Lonnie. The tree that had been hit was some distance from any others and not afire. It didn't appear there would be any forest fire to worry about.

"It's burning itself out," Lonnie said. "But whoever is in that car there's got to be a goner. No one could live through that much hell."

"He was dead before we smashed into the tree," Ron Bowdrie's voice was surprisingly strong. The lawman was leaning against a large rock a few dozen feet to the left. Blood was seeping through fingers grasped to his face and dripping on the ground. "When that bullet hit the windshield, the last thing I saw was the top of Frank's skull being blown away. Some of the flying glass has got me blinded, boys."

"This fire ain't gonna spread none," Woody said. Only a

few scant tongues of flame licking outward from underneath the DeSoto were noticeable. He stepped close and studied the charred corpse that was still in the passenger seat, staring straight ahead at a bull's-eye hole in the windshield.

Ron Bowdrie had been right about the damage the bullet had done. He could see the man's scorched brains. Then an overpowering stench came drifting on hot air from the open window and struck him like a fist. The smell of burning human flesh was indescribably nauseating. The sickening sweet odor from the still-sizzling body he knew he would remember forever. Fighting down the urge to retch, he staggered over to Lonnie and Ron.

"Ain't nobody needs to worry themselves any about saving the man in the car," Woody said over building bile. "Let's see how bad Slow Ron's been hurt, then we'd better get him to a doc."

Lonnie ran to his truck and came back carrying a green metal box with a red cross painted on it, causing Woody to wonder what else the scrapper could come up with in a pinch. He set the first aid kit alongside the bleeding lawman, popped open the latch and said in a surprisingly gentle voice for such a large man, "I'm going to open a bottle of boric acid solution, dump it on some gauze and daub away the blood. This is the only way I can see how much damage that flying glass did."

Ron lowered his crimson hands. "I'm keeping my eyes closed. Take your time and don't do more damage than what's already done."

Woody knelt to watch the proceedings. Lonnie carefully and deftly used one wad of gauze after another until he finally turned his gaze to Woody and shook his head sadly. He pointed to a large shard of glass that was likely embedded an inch or more into the lawman's right eye.

"I think you'll be just fine," Lonnie lied. "But to be on the safe side and guard your eyesight, I'm going to put cotton pads over your eyes and wrap gauze around your head to hold them in place. The doc in Silver City will fix you up. Don't you worry about a thing."

"I don't need to see to know who it was that killed Officer Keller and tried to get me too," Ron said while Lonnie worked at taping thick padding over the marshal's bleeding eyes. "I intend to see him fry in the electric chair for what he done."

"Now you just stay calm," Woody said. "We heard the shot, but never saw anybody. There'll be plenty of time to sort things out once you're healed up."

"I can talk on a phone." Ron winced when Lonnie washed out a deep cut on his forehead with antiseptic before taping a strip of gauze over it. "There's only one man had any reason to do this and I'm gonna have the state police come and arrest the bastard."

"Don't go off half-cocked," Woody said. "I'm telling you we didn't see who shot that bullet and from what you said, you didn't either."

"Pat Gunn had the motive and there's no good reason to look past him. When we get him in jail, he'll confess just to cut a deal to keep from frying. Lowlife crooks like him are all yellow to the core."

Woody could not hold the remains of lunch in his stomach any longer. He jumped up, bolted to the far side of Lonnie's truck, to heave in the narrow bar ditch. The smell of roasting human flesh was terrible enough to deal with besides having to deal with the thought that his best friend was, at the very least, a murder suspect. And until just a few minutes ago, the day had been going really good.

"I'll help you get Ron into the cab of your truck," Woody said, wiping spittle from his lips with the back of his hand. "Then you can haul him to Silver City without me going along."

"I recognize that voice of yours, Woody Johnson," Ron Bowdrie growled with building rage. "Pat Gunn and you are thick as thieves. Damn crooks the both of you. Won't do you no good to try and help him now that there's a dead lawman here in Wisdom. When a state policeman gets murdered, there ain't no place for anyone involved to hide."

Lonnie shrugged his massive shoulders. "I reckon it would be best for me to haul him in by myself."

"I can walk, dammit," Ron grunted as he hoisted his bulk erect. He made a few testing movements with his limbs. "Aside from having a little glass in my eyes, I'm damn fine." He held out a bloody hand. "Now if someone'll help me get in whatever they're driving, I'd like to get to Silver City and a telephone."

Woody stood aside and watched in silence as Lonnie helped the wounded marshal into his truck, turned to the big rig around and roared off to the west. He then broke into a hurried run back to his cabin and his Model A pickup. His mind was blank on what to say or do when he located Pat, but there was no way the theater owner could have killed anyone.

The biggest problem, as he saw it, would be attempting to convince everyone else of that fact.

"Oliver," Harriet Jordan exclaimed to her husband as he barely managed to avoid being forced off a steep cliff. "That truck driver nearly hit us head-on!"

"He's the man that's been scrapping out mines for metal. I don't know what his big hurry is, he didn't even have a full load on that truck of his."

"I hope he doesn't cause anyone an accident."

"On this road it would be easy for him to do."

The old woman hesitated. "I think it might have been better if he had hit us."

"Not yet, Mama. We have to honor our promise to Robert first."

"I know, dear." Her voice was dry and emotionless as a sirocco coming off desert sand. "I know."

CHAPTER NINE

Pat Gunn was behind the concession counter of the Starlight, fishing crickets out of a big tin of popcorn. The pesky chirpers had not called the canister home for very long, leading him to believe the yellow kernels would still pop up just fine.

He grabbed up the last offender, dashed it to the floor and ground it flat under the sole of his shoe. Then he clucked his tongue when he noticed little back reminders of the invasion strewn among the popcorn. It would be a while before he could fire up the popper. Then would be the time to worry over trifles. He shook the can and grinned with satisfaction when all he now saw were nice clean kernels of corn. This time he remembered to tamp the lid on tight before placing it beneath the counter.

The long red cooler next to the wall was packed with squat bottles of Coca-Cola, the popular nickel drink that he happily sold for a dime. He took one out and popped the lid in the opener. He took a sip, then began thumbing through the past week's mail.

Bills could always be looked at later. The letter postmarked in Chicago with no return address was what he had been hoping to have show up. He carefully inserted his pocketknife under the flap and slit it open. Inside was a beautiful red "C" mileage ration sticker to place on the windshield of his Studebaker. Also enclosed were skillfully forged credentials claiming that Patrick Callahan Gunn was an ordained Methodist minister. Preachers, along with doctors, hospital workers, mail carriers and government officials, were eligible for unlimited gasoline purchases.

Pat did not foresee any difficulties in passing himself off as a Methodist. He had actually attended services in a church of that calling many times growing up as a youth in Illinois. He knew the names of a lot of hymns. A Bible on the dash, along with a well-chosen quote or two from it, would get him out of most any fix he could envision.

What he hated to face, starting in December, was to try and survive on the four gallons of gasoline a week that the gray ration stamp issued the average person would allow.

Woody's cabin was just above town, but six miles away by road. A single trip up that steep mountain and back consumed nearly an entire gallon.

There were, of course some difficulties to be faced. He would be forced to change the windshield and drive to Silver City to buy fuel. Should he show up at Slow Ron's station to buy gasoline on a red sticker, the fat lawman would certainly question his elevation of status and cause him problems. But he already had the extra windshield and it did not appear to be a lot of work to exchange them. Besides, an occasional trip to Silver city would be a nice diversion.

Phylo Norton was such a skilled counterfeiter there was no reason to concern himself that anyone would question the validity of that sticker. Then again, Phylo *had* spent several years in Joliet when he accidentally put Grover Cleveland's picture on the wrong series of twenty-dollar bills.

He reassured himself that no one would likely inspect a ration sticker as closely as they would a double sawbuck, and the fifteen dollars he had sent Phylo was a good investment.

The big, ticking regulator clock on the far wall above a

poster for *Casablanca*, the most profitable movie he had ever shown, indicated it to be almost four o'clock. Normally he did not imbibe until after five, but with a World War raging on these were not normal times. He chugged the remains of the Coke and headed out the door.

Woody Johnson's black pickup came around the sharp turn at the lower end of town nearly on two wheels. Pat thought this was odd. He had never really known his friend to get into a rush over much of anything. Then again, last night Woody *had* spent over an entire dollar buying drinks and visiting with Carla. He was right about the war changing everyone in one manner or the other.

Pat turned and locked the door before going to find out what had his friend in a dither. He couldn't afford having kids sneak in to eat up the remaining candy bars or drink his supply of Coca-Cola. It struck him like a jolt of electricity when he remembered there were not any children in Wisdom. Not anymore. They had all gone with their parents to other towns. The large four-room schoolhouse was boarded up, silent as the stones it was built from.

He missed the laughter of kids. This time of day, on their way home from school, the little ones would swarm in front of the Starlight to point excitedly at posters and the marquee while yammering excitedly. Kids always loved moving pictures and endlessly talked about them, along with the stars, be they villains or heroes.

Those sweet children were often the only reason a lot of grownups ever parted with money to visit his theater. Now a simple government edict innocuously called L-208 had swept them all from the town of Wisdom like a scouring wind.

Woody slammed his foot down hard on what remained of the Model A's brakes in a futile attempt to bring the speeding pickup to a quick halt. The piercing sound of tortured metal grinding against metal echoed off craggy cliffs before fading into the distance.

Pat shook his head sadly and walked the hundred feet or so to where his friend's truck had finally ground to a stop in front of Joe Godfrey's closed restaurant and bakery.

"You're either going to have to buy some new brakes or learn to slow down a tad," Pat said, wearing his usual smile.

Woody jumped out, leaving the door open. His agonized expression spoke of tragedy. "There's been a killing on the highway just below where you turn into my place."

"A killing!" Pat was aghast. "You've got to mean a car wreck. Lots of folks have gone over a cliff on that road and not lived through it."

"No Pat, this is a murder, plain and simple." Woody looked around to assure himself they were alone. "It was most likely that arson investigator Ron went to meet. Whoever it was had a rifle bullet blow away the top of his skull. Ron was driving him in the police cruiser. Ron took a face-full of glass from the shot and crashed into a tree. Lonnie Dillman, the metal scrapper, hauled him to the doc in Silver City. I don't know if he'll be blind or not, but aside from his eyes he ain't bad hurt. The car caught fire and I'll guarantee there's one cooked goose up on that mountain."

"My God!" Pat exclaimed. "Pearl's still got a phone that's turned on. We'd better go call the county sheriff. Sam Sinrod will have to come out and investigate."

"Yeah," Woody said with a sigh. "I kinda figured on calling him. He'll need to bring along a meat wagon, too."

Both men were so agitated they did not notice the Jordans approach, until the battered old station wagon they drove sputtered to a stop.

"There's been a terrible wreck this side of Angel's Roost

Pass." Oliver spoke, staring blandly ahead. He could have been describing the weather. "A car hit a tree and caught fire. Mama and I thought we saw a dead body inside."

"I just came from there," Woody said calmly. "We're going to call the sheriff out."

Oliver said, "Ronnie Bowdrie is the local law. We didn't notice him at the gas station. Maybe he's at the firehouse."

"That burned car you saw is Slow Ron's police cruiser." Woody began fishing for his smoking tobacco. "He's getting hauled into the doc's by the fellow scrapping out the mines. Ron's hurt, but likely not too bad. You folks are right about one fellow being killed."

"Let us know how poor Ronnie is doing when you hear," the silver-haired woman said, keeping her gaze ahead. "He's a good man and he was a friend to our son."

"That's why that trucker was in such a hurry, Mama," Oliver said to no one as he let out the clutch. The old station wagon gave out a groan and continued on its way through town, tires crunching on gravel now. President Roosevelt's New Deal, aided by the state, had stopped paving at the city limits.

"That's a pure miracle," Pat said once the old couple had gone.

"Why's that?"

"I've been here for years and that's the first time I ever heard *anyone* say a good word about Slow Ron."

"Their kid grew up with him; they used to play together. Reckon that's how he came to take."

"Yeah, well since you've got your car out, I'll ride up to the Happy Eagle with you." Pat walked around and climbed in. "Be a shame to waste gas."

Woody turned on the ignition switch, reached with his foot for the starter then hesitated. Usually his friend was quicker on the uptake than he appeared to be in this instance. "You *do* know that investigator was coming here to check out your house burning. I'd venture him getting shot just before he hit town might have a tendency to cast a shadow of suspicion on you doing it. Ron ain't being that generous. I can say that with certainty."

Pat's eyes took on an odd, faraway glaze and his face lost all expression. "I know that's how the law will think, Woody. I know it all too well. All I can do is tell the truth. I was working in the Starlight all day long and hope like hell they'll believe me."

"I'll go make the call to Silver City. You might want to take this time to look through your place." He hesitated. "You know, maybe there's a gun that would be best dropped down a mine shaft or something."

Pat kept his eyes forward. "I don't even own a firearm of any kind. And I don't have any idea who shot that poor fellow. I didn't want him dead, I wanted the man to confirm I had an accidental fire. With the hubbub that's likely coming now, it'll be weeks before I get my insurance money."

"If Slow Ron has any say in the matter, a few weeks from now you'll be strapped in an electric chair spewing smoke out of your ears."

"Most lawmen operate on evidence. I just hope they'll do their own checking and not rely on Ron's rantings."

"Let's go make that call," Woody spun the starter. "I swear Pat, you're the most optimistic SOB I've ever run across. Here you are up to your neck in horse shit and you're grinning and looking around for the great horse that left it here as if it's some gift from heaven."

"A person don't need to fret any before the fact. Put this clunker in gear. I could sure use a scotch and hailstones."

★ ★ ★ ★ ★

Irene Chapman stumbled to the window of the Bloated Goat. She had heard screeching brakes along with car motors running. The entire day had passed without this much excitement.

"Anybody coming our way?" Fred asked.

"I don't see 'em if they are. Woody's truck's heading off towards Pearl's joint."

"That's gratitude for you. I bought firewood off that man for years. Now that we need his business, he starts drinking at the Happy Eagle."

"This town'll be booming again soon." Irene returned to her mint julep. "You'll see."

Fred flipped the top off another bottle of beer and plopped down next to the radio. A rerun of "The Eddie Cantor Show" was on. He wasn't paying much attention to the show, but it was better than listening to the silence.

"Yes, dear," he mumbled. "I'm sure you're right." He turned up the volume on the Crosley and drank his beer. There was really nothing else that needed to be done.

CHAPTER TEN

"Get a poke," Nero shrieked at Woody and Pat when they strode through the door of the Happy Eagle. "Bugger 'em, bugger 'em!"

"Ah, go lay a hard-boiled egg," Woody growled at the parrot on his way to the bar.

Pearl stood smiling behind the long mahogany counter, wearing a very tight fitting and revealing green dress. Spinner sat on a stool, twirling his coin, sipping a short beer. Alvin was stroking out a soft tune on the upright piano. Carla sat alone at a table, drinking whiskey and soda. This night was shaping up to be a carbon copy of the night before, or at least it had been up until Pearl read the foreboding expression on both men's faces.

"Things aren't jake tonight, are they boys?" she asked. "What's happened?"

Woody tossed down a silver dollar that rang like a bell when it struck the bar. "Give us a drink, then I'll tell what I know before I borrow the phone and call the sheriff. I reckon the drink'll be plenty helpful. Leastwise it will be for me."

The old miner's bottle of Carling Black Label beer was empty when he had finished telling of the late afternoon's events. In spite of the harrowing day, he felt better when Carla came over to stand by his side.

Pearl chewed on her lower lip. After a moment she nodded her head at the black telephone behind the bar. "Make the call, Woody, but don't have the law meet you *here,* for Pete's sake. I can't afford to be paying any bribe money the way things are these days."

Pat gave an understanding nod. "The sheriff can meet us at the Starlight. It'll take him a couple of hours to reach here, even blowing his siren. There's no rush."

"That's not a great idea," Woody said firmly. "The first thing the law'll do is toss your place."

"Then the sooner they get it out of their system, the better."

Spinner wheezed. "Pat, you ought to listen up some here. The law's business is to throw folks in jail, just to close the case." He fought for enough wind to continue. "Being guilty ain't a requirement for getting locked up."

Alvin, who had quit his piano playing to listen, said, "My grandfather was friends to a man that got hung for murder over in Arizona. While the poor fellow was still dangling from the gallows, an Arizona ranger came driving into town with the real killer who had confessed. I think that would be enough to make me skittish when it comes to dealing with the law."

Carla opined, "The only difference I've noted between a crook and a lawman is a badge."

"I prefer the crooks," Pearl said. "They're more trustworthy."

"Well, what a cheery group of friends I've got," Pat said. "It does my heart good to have such a great bunch of supporters. Woody, make your call, I need the gaiety."

"Gotta happen sooner or later." Woody walked behind the bar, grabbed the receiver and stuck it to his ear. "The line's busy." He hung up.

Pearl gave a sigh. "That's Big Jimmy Lyons, he's a rancher who lives clear over in Wildcat Canyon. That man likes to prattle on worse than a politician stumping for an election." She picked up the phone. "Put a sock in it, Percy

Pants, we need to call the law."

After a long moment of listening to the receiver, Pearl nodded agreeably and handed it to Woody. "The operator's coming on."

The old man asked to be connected with the sheriff's office in Silver City. He heard a click on the line while the phone was ringing, confirming his surmise that Big Jimmy Lyons would have plenty to talk about real soon.

Woody spoke, his face hard as steel, giving the facts as he knew them in short, blunt sentences. The conversation took only moments.

Returning to his seat Woody announced, "Well folks, the cavalry's heading our way."

Spinner gave an incredulous look at the sweaty, brown bottle of beer Pearl had set in front of him. He could not remember the last time he had had a full beer to drink. "What's this for?"

"Pat and the whole darn town of Wisdom have trouble coming." She lit a cigarette while pouring herself a gin. "We've got time for a little party first. I'm buying until the time comes for Pat to go meet the law."

Woody felt a sensation like a trickle of warm oil down his back when Carla wrapped a soft arm around his waist and ushered him to a table.

Alvin set a fresh beer Pearl had brought him on the table by the piano, wrestled his legs into position and began playing "Someone to Watch Over Me."

The tone inside the Happy Eagle Bar turned subdued. The professor played only soft, mellow tunes. Some wondered and worried about what new grievances were about to strike their moribund little mountain town. Others simply marveled that the madam of a brothel was giving away free drinks.

Pat sat at the bar, Pearl by his side. They sipped their drinks and murmured candy whispers that can only be spoken between a man and a woman. For weeks now they had sought each other's company every evening. Sometimes, Pearl would give out a schoolgirl giggle and squeeze his hand. Every single night they had parted to go their own ways without so much as a peck on the cheek.

No one in Wisdom was more of a keen observer of human nature than Alvin Kent. He understood that Pat and the madam were older and likely careful for being hurt in the distant past by other, now faceless, lovers. Barriers built of painful memories were sturdy, yet could be chipped away by kindness and love over time, like running water moves mountains to the sea, unnoticeably slow, yet constantly effecting change, day by day. Eventually, the changes wrought could no longer be denied. Alvin blinked wetness from his eyes to focus on his piano playing. He often had trouble keeping from thinking of himself, and just how much more alone he was than anyone left in this dying town.

From the corner of Pearl's eye, she paid scant attention to Woody and Carla, who sat together at the most distant table, except to notice they spent more time talking than drinking. This was agreeable and saved her money.

Pearl could not help but wonder how much longer her only girl would stay. It was puzzling why Carla had stayed this long. All of the younger, voluptuous working girls that had so successfully mined the miners had seen the handwriting on the wall. But Carla thought of herself as old and plain. With proper makeup and attire, the girl could continue in the business for years. What kept Carla's spirits down was a mystery. Anyway, Pearl's interest was held by Pat Gunn these days. At present, the man badly needed looking after. That was a certainty.

Time passed all too quickly. Pat forced his gaze from sparkling emerald eyes to the loudly ticking oak clock on the wall next to the inviting archway adorned with silky red curtains. He shook his head sadly, gave a final swirl to the few remaining hailstones in his glass, slugged down the watered dregs of what had been excellent scotch, clucked his tongue worriedly and said, "Pearl darling, I guess I can't put this off any longer."

The scraping sound of Pat sliding back his stool to stand took Woody's attention. The miner bent over the table and whispered something in Carla's ear that caused her to laugh happily. She got up, stepped around the small round table and pulled a startled Woody to his feet. Then she wrapped both arms around his neck and pressed her ruby lips to his. The kiss was full to the mouth, long and deep.

Woody pulled away, wheezing worse than Spinner did when he made those loud gurgling sounds that caused people to try and remember the undertaker's phone number.

"I, I didn't mean to embarrass you," Carla said haltingly.

Woody composed himself. "If that's called getting embarrassed, we'll need do it more often, so's I can get over it." He swallowed hard when he turned toward Pat. "Let's get on with this before I start spending money I can't afford."

Spinner said, "Boys, if I can get a ride to the Starlight, I'd appreciate it. It's occurred to me that Slow Ron's wife probably doesn't know he's been hurt. Be a shame for her to find out from a stranger." He took a moment to catch his breath. "They live just a couple of blocks or so from my place."

"You're right, Spinner," Woody said. "That's the problem with being married to Slow Ron, that wife of his is always forgot about because everyone's always too busy complaining about him. I'll drop you off in front of the gas station. That way you can fill her in on the news then have a downhill walk all the way home."

Pearl was by Pat's side before he realized it. The heady, sweet essence of cherry blossoms in springtime begged him to tarry.

"I'll come back and let you know what Sheriff Sinrod had to say—if I can." Pat's voice was tight.

In less than a heartbeat of time, Pearl had swept Pat into an embrace. She left a crimson smear on his cheek, the first time she had kissed a man since—

"You get back here real soon," she said.

Pat nodded as he turned to the door. After a moment of waiting for Spinner to shuffle along with them, they were gone.

Alvin noticed the only two ladies in the Happy Eagle had misty eyes. He turned to the upright and began playing "Danny Boy." There was no good reason he could think of to be cheerful.

CHAPTER ELEVEN

"Damn it, there's nothing in this whole world that smells worse than someone who's been burned to a crisp." Doctor Bryce Whitlock, coroner of Grant County, stepped back from the charred DeSoto, playing the beam of his flashlight over the corpse. "From the looks of things this man wasn't bothered any by the fire."

"No sir," Sam Sinrod said, keeping his distance alongside the Chevrolet cruiser that was idling with its headlights on to help illuminate the scene. "The man who called it in said Marshal Bowdrie told him he saw the top of the man's head get blown away by a bullet that hit the windshield."

"Where's this marshal at?"

"Some truck driver hauled him to the hospital in Silver City. He got shards of flying glass in his eyes. I reckon we must have passed them on the road."

The coroner snorted and moved the angle of the light. "Possibly the bullet may have gone into the trunk and lodged there. There's no hole in the back window where it went on through."

The sheriff cocked his head and looked uphill to where the road disappeared into darkness. "That being the case, the shooter had to be considerably higher than the road for the bullet to angle down like that."

"Come daylight, I want you and your deputies to go over both sides of this road with a fine tooth comb. I mean go out as far as a half mile. Concentrate on the high ground. The shell casing may very well be lying in plain sight. Make sure no one touches it. Fingerprints solve more crimes all the time."

"Yes sir, Doctor Whitlock. My men know what to do. This dead man, well he's likely a state police arson investigator. If that's the case, by tomorrow night we'll be up to our undershorts in red tape. We can also plan on most anybody in Santa Fe that wears a badge showing up to cause us irritation."

"Wonderful, simply wonderful." The coroner tucked the flashlight under his arm and lit a cigarette. "The more government we have to contend with, the harder this case will be to solve. By the way, sheriff, how did you come to think this man's a state lawman?"

"Marshal Bowdrie brought an arson investigator from Santa Fe by earlier today. Came promenading into my office like we were old friends and introduced him to me as Frank—somebody, I can't recollect the last name. Bowdrie said he was out to prove that Pat Gunn, the fellow who owns the picture show in Wisdom, burned down his own home for the insurance money."

The coroner's wry smile was masked by shadows. Bryce Whitlock had been out of medical school only four years and most considered him quite young for the office, which he had run for unopposed. A great many physicians had answered the nation's call for doctors after Pearl Harbor and were now serving in the armed forces. A mild case of diabetes was the only thing that had kept him from joining the military.

"I would view anyone burning down an insured house in Wisdom," Doctor Whitlock said, "as having too much good sense to kill an arson investigator. That would be the act of an idiot. Arson crimes are the hardest of all to solve and get a conviction on. Almost certainly the results of an investigation would have stated, 'Fire of unknown origin.' Norbert Pike would never file on anything that petty, anyway. The district attorney wants folks voting for him, not upset with him."

"Yes sir, Doc. But the facts are, somebody went and killed this man. Getting away with calling this death a suicide seems like a long shot."

"That much is obvious." The coroner genuinely liked Sheriff Sinrod. Sam wasn't much older than he; both men sported pencil-thin moustaches and kept their hair slicked back with Wildroot Cream Oil. He also appreciated the sheriff's occasional dark humor. Things like toasted corpses with the tops of their heads missing made a sense of humor mandatory for anyone wishing to keep a grip on sanity. "I just want to make sure the right person gets convicted."

"Yes sir, so do I. My men will be scouring for that shell casing come the crack of dawn. I'll have Neil, Bob and Rodney here. Burke, I'll have to keep in the office. Having all the law two hours from town might invite trouble." He stepped closer. "What do we do with the body?"

The doctor looked about and sighed. "If that corpse turns out to be a lawman, every move we make will get picked apart. Keeping that in mind; have the wrecker hook onto the car and tow it back with the body where it's at. I'll take some measurements and photos in the light of morning before I do the autopsy. I want to confirm an ID before calling the capital and kicking that hornet's nest.

"That will buy us a little time to do our own investigation. I really am hoping the slug is in the trunk or embedded in what's left of the back seat. Then we can pinpoint the caliber of rifle we're looking for."

"There'll doubtless be a few thousand like it hereabouts."

"You'll probably be right, Sam, but only one person will have used a rifle to kill someone. That's how we solve crimes, by narrowing the field one piece of evidence at a time."

"Just like Sam Spade or Sherlock Holmes would do."

"I'm glad we both like detective novels. I have a gut feeling this case is going to have some twists and turns before it's over."

"We can be certain if a bunch of idiots from the capital comes here, they'll finger everyone for this crime, from Pat Gunn to John Wilkes Booth and Adolph Hitler. I'd really like to have a good handle on this before they show up."

"I'll stall as long as I can. Motion down the wrecker and hearse. Thornton will be mighty relieved not having to haul a burnt body back inside with him. Once you've got everyone lined out, I'll ride into Wisdom with you. I'm anxious as you are to see what folks there have to say."

The sheriff flashed the lights on his cruiser twice to signal the men he had kept away from the scene that it was all right for them to approach. He then stepped over to the doctor and bummed a cigarette. After lighting the smoke, he motioned with the still burning match to the DeSoto; an evil smirk on his face was silhouetted by flickering flames.

"If the man in that car was to turn out to be the theater owner, it'd make this case a lot easier to solve."

Doctor Whitlock lowered his eyebrows. "Why's that?"

"We'd have our smoking Gunn."

"Pat, when did you get infested with religion and become a dad-gummed preacher?" Woody was thumbing through the mail his friend has left lying on top of the counter to while away time waiting for the sheriff. "That red gas ration stamp's cuter than a gnat's eyebrow, too."

"A friend of mine sent it to me as a joke." Pat marched over and grabbed the papers. "Phylo doesn't realize things like this can cause a man grief."

In a brief moment, Pat Gunn's minister's diploma, along with his beautiful unlimited gasoline stamp, had been turned into ashes.

"Shame to burn those up like you did," Woody said with a wink. "That friend of yours put a lot of work into funning you."

"Oh, Phylo's a real card alright. If he takes to turning out ration stickers, he'll have more time on his hands than he's bargained for. Lawmen aren't noted for a sense of humor when it comes to things like that. After all, there's a war on."

"We all know things are getting tougher. I sure would've like to have had use of that red sticker to buy gas for my air compressor. That big old Buda engine'll burn my entire four-gallon weekly ration in a couple hours of drilling. And it takes me a full day just to drill out a single round."

"The war will be over in a few months. You couldn't sell any ore nowadays, even if you did accidentally happen to blast into some. It's against the law to mine gold."

"There's also laws against burning down houses and claiming to be a Methodist preacher, but I ain't noticed any of that slowing *you* down—"

Woody grew silent when a flash of headlights twinkled in the tall glass windows. "You ever met this sheriff?" he asked as the late model Chevrolet with a big round light on its roof pulled to a stop in front of the theater.

"No," Pat said watching two slender young men climb out of the cruiser. "But it looks like I'm fixing to get to know him a lot better than I'd ever planned on."

The first man through the door of the Starlight sported a

neat brown uniform. A revolver tucked in a black leather holster dangled from a thick belt that also held a shiny set of handcuffs. A silver star pinned over his heart glistened in the flickering light from the marquee. Pat wondered why any sheriff would ever hire such a young kid for a deputy. The next fellow inside wasn't much older; he had a factory-made cigarette dangling from his lips and was dressed in a tweed suit with a natty blue and red tie clasped with a diamond stickpin to the front of the whitest shirt Pat had seen in years. A set of gold cufflinks assured this other man was no policeman. He did, however, fit the appearance of a Chicago pimp to perfection.

"Mister Woodrow Johnson?" the uniformed man inquired, taking his hat off with one hand while keeping the other at the ready for a handshake with whoever answered.

Woody grimaced. "Call me Woody, officer. My sweet mother, rest her soul, had fond hopes of my turning out to be a Methodist minister, but I chose a calling that requires a less formal name."

"Then Woody it is." The young officer grasped the miner's calloused hand. "I'm Sam Sinrod, sheriff of Grant County." He gave a head wag to his stylish companion. "This is Doctor Bryce Whitlock, he's our county coroner."

Pat had difficulty recovering from the fact that two boys appeared to spearhead the law. It was a strain, but he made his introductions without comment on their youth and inexperience.

"I'm surprised," the sheriff said to Pat, "to see the place lit up and that you're still showing motion pictures. I'd heard most folks had left for greener pastures after the mines closed. The W. C. Fields movie you have coming is a lot of fun to watch. I've seen it twice."

Doctor Whitlock decided not to comment on Pat

Gunn's lack of spelling ability or the quality of the latest moving pictures and get on with business. The drive back to Silver City took at least two hours.

"Gentlemen," the coroner said, "we've inspected the scene and we have a definite homicide on our hands. There's good reason to believe the man who was shot and then burned is an arson investigator the local marshal was bringing here to Wisdom to investigate a house fire." He focused on Pat. "I believe the house in question belonged to you, Mister Gunn."

"That's right," Pat said quickly using the most innocent tone he could muster. "I can't explain Slow Ron getting such a bee in his bonnet with me except for the fact that he wants to make a name for himself to get a state lawman's job. I was miles away at Woody's place, drinking a bit of scotch when we both first noticed the smoke. I'd been there for hours."

Doctor Whitlock took a final puff on the stub of his cigarette. "*Who* is Slow Ron?"

Sam chuckled. "I've heard Ronald Bowdrie called that many times, Doc. The local marshal is also chief of the fire department. Most people in Wisdom claim a crippled turtle moves faster than Bowdrie does. Most generally, he gets to a fire in time to squirt water on the foundation. He's applied to the sheriff's department for a job lots of times, but so far no one's been desperate enough to hire him."

Woody handed the doctor an ashtray. "You're right that Slow Ron ain't a cherished citizen in Wisdom. He makes his wife do all the work of running their gas station and most believe he beats on her, too. But I'd still be obliged to know how his eyes are. He got a big piece of glass stuck in one of them. I also remember he done a lot of yelling about that man who was killed being a state lawman. If that's the case, I'd reckon all kinds of crap will be hitting the fan until the killer is found."

"That's putting it mildly," the sheriff said. "And yes, there's good reason to believe the murdered man is a state policeman."

"I'm going to do an autopsy on the body in the morning." The coroner tapped out a Chesterfield from a fresh pack. "When that's done, and we've established the man's identity beyond any reasonable doubt, I'll phone Santa Fe. That'll take me until lunchtime. The day after tomorrow, if we don't know who shot that officer by then, this town will be crawling with lawmen."

Sheriff Sinrod placed his hands on his hips and glared at first Pat, then Woody. "So gentlemen, I put it to you; we *are* going to solve this murder. If either one of you knows anything about this crime, things will go a lot easier for you if you spill it."

Doctor Whitlock added sternly, "Speak up men. You live here. If there's anybody who would've killed that man, you'd be the likely ones to know who it is."

Woody snorted, "Hells bells, there ain't no one in Wisdom, aside of Pat here, who'd have any reason to be bothered by that man showing up." He noticed his friend's shocked expression. "Of course, Pat was here working in his theater when it happened and had nothing to do with any shooting."

"Can anyone verify that?" Sinrod asked, his gray eyes glaring now.

"I don't know," Pat shuffled his feet. "I honestly don't. There's not an awful lot of people here these days. Since I lost my house, I've been living here in the theater. This morning, I changed some light bulbs and lettered the marquee. Spinner Olsson saw me and, oh yeah, the Jordans drove by. After lunch I took a short nap then worked on my mail, but never went outside once."

"That anybody saw," the sheriff added.

"Yessir," Pat said. "It's a fact I don't recall seeing a single soul until Woody showed up in a frenzy. Then we drove up to Pearl's and called you. She's likely got the only working phone left in town aside of Slow Ron's."

"Does this Pearl have a last name?"

"It's Dunbar, Sheriff." Pat clucked his tongue. "She owns a nice little workingman's bar a few blocks up the canyon."

Sam Sinrod's knowing expression spoke that he knew full well about the goings-on at the Happy Eagle. "I may want to question her, is all."

Doctor Whitlock said, "From the looks of things that man was killed with a high powered rifle." His gaze flicked from Pat to Woody. "Either of you two own one of those?"

"I don't own a weapon of any kind," Pat said. "Not much need for one in the theater business."

"There's a thirty-thirty Winchester and a double barreled twelve gauge up at my place," Woody said. "Hunting gives me a lot of my grub."

"Do you mind if we look around some?" Sinrod asked, facing Pat.

"Not at all." The theater owner had expected this. "Poke around all you want."

"Thank you, Mister Gunn, I may do that later on. For now I need to get the doctor back to Silver City. Tomorrow's going to be a busy day." The sheriff nodded to Woody. "If I don't make it back here tomorrow, I'll phone Pearl and let her know how Bowdrie's getting along. I assume you drop by her place on occasion."

"Yes sir, I do—on occasion," Woody sounded hoarse.

Without further words, the two lawmen turned and were gone.

"What do you make of that?" Woody asked.

"I'm their prime suspect in a murder, that's a fact. Aside from that cheerful news, I went and burned up some things I needn't to have done. Let's go up to Pearl's and have ourselves another drink. By the way, for being so darn helpful in pointing out to the law I'm the only one in the whole blame world who'd want to shoot that poor fellow—you're buying."

A stab of guilt gave Woody an expression of cold despair. "I'm mighty sorry about that. I didn't think before I opened my trap. That sheriff went and rattled me somewhat more than I'd expected."

"That's all right. I'm telling the truth. That should be enough to keep me out of trouble."

"I'm sure things will work out fine." Woody hesitated as they stepped outside. "But I'm still going to buy you a drink."

Pat's usual grin was back. "Buck up, my friend. With any good luck Pearl's still giving out free booze."

"You're an optimist, I'll hand you that. Let's hop in my truck and go see if you're right about Pearl still acting nutty."

As Woody's Model A sputtered to life, Pat turned and looked out the back window of the pickup at the cheerful flashing lights of the Starlight's marquee. It was a promise, a balm in Gilead. Just like the hero in one of his favorite movies, he would get through this. Pat kept staring at those twinkling, wonderful lights until they became but a tiny glimmer, persevering against the gloom of night.

CHAPTER TWELVE

Doctor Whitlock loved the blazing New Mexico sunrises. The dreary steel mill city of Pittsburgh was the only home he had known until he had received his medical degree and accepted a position in the small mountain town of Silver City.

In contrast to Pennsylvania's constantly smoke-filled skies, fog, bitter cold weather, along with milling crowds, here a man could bathe in silence while watching the Almighty paint glowing masterpieces upon the walls of Heaven.

He sighed when he remembered Father Lujan, the frail old Spanish priest who had been one of his first patients upon his arrival here. The old padre was dying of stomach cancer. Every morning the venerable priest would be found sitting at an east window of the hospital, facing the distant Kneeling Nun, a towering pinnacle of rock that overlooks the sprawling Santa Rita copper mine.

"The fire of God comes from out of the east," Father Lujan had said. "It crosses the skies unseen until the Maker calls it home at the end of its journey. There is nothing anyone can do to stop this, nor should they try. My own journey is ended; I accept my fate as I accept the sunrise and its setting. I await the journey to come with much eagerness."

Father Lujan undertook his final journey, leaving behind a smile on his emaciated face. To this day, every sunrise was "the fire of God."

This morning, Doctor Whitlock could savor the display but briefly. More earthy and distasteful duties demanded his attention.

The roasted corpse inside of the DeSoto had been extracted for him to autopsy. He had used up a full roll of film in his Contax camera to preserve the scene for the record before ordering the body moved. The coroner had been unable to find traces of gunpowder residue around the bullet hole in the windshield. This would have indicated that the shooter was within a few feet of the car. The finding came as no surprise, but in a case such as this one every possibility had to be checked out and documented. He had already surmised the bullet had traveled from some distance.

He took a small green bottle of camphor from his pocket, smeared a generous helping under his nose, then offered it to the wide-eyed young man who worked in the impound yard.

"What's that for?" the man asked.

"It cuts down on the smell. If I were you," the coroner said, "I'd smear on a lot of it under your nose before you pop the trunk open, which is what I want done now."

"I can handle it."

Doctor Whitlock returned the bottle to his pocket. A few moments later, the trunk lid was raised and the young man was a good fifty feet away, leaning on a fence for support, heaving up his breakfast.

The coroner went to the front of the car and sighted from the bullet hole in the windshield along a wood stick he had propped up in the seat to indicate where the top of Frank Keller's head had been blown away. The officer was shorter than he had originally thought. The angle taken by the slug was steeper than he had anticipated it being.

There was no longer any doubt as to the dead man's

identity. A charred wallet held a quite legible ID, along with a badge. There had also been the seemingly inevitable photograph of a smiling, pretty woman holding two beaming children. Surprisingly, the picture was barely scorched. Briefly, he had wondered to whom in Santa Fe would fall the sad task of informing the family. Then he focused back on the job at hand. He had to have his facts in order to prepare for the maelstrom that would be certainly now be coming.

"Anything new to report?"

The coroner had not heard Sam Sinrod return after taking the dead man's wallet to his office for safekeeping. "No, but now that you're here I can use your help."

The sheriff motioned to the young man who was still gasping for breath and attempting to heave. "It looks like Wes isn't doing a lot of assisting."

"That's the penalty one pays for ignoring sound medical advice. Go around to the open trunk. I know pretty well how high the bullet struck; now we need to figure out how much to the side."

"Why do you get to stay in the fresh air?" Sam took a deep breath and poked his head inside the trunk. Enough of the seat and back liner had burned away to give a mediocre view through to the coroner.

"It says I can on my medical diploma. Quit sniveling and move your hand to the right. Keep your eyes peeled for a hole or bulge."

"I know we're looking for a bullet. But, I can't see or feel a thing."

Whitlock snorted. "Try searching to *my* right. About a foot up."

"By golly," the sheriff's voice was elated. "There's not only a bulge here, the dad-blasted slug's sticking halfway out of the seat back." He hesitated. "Don't say it. I won't touch it until you get back here."

"Go ahead and pull it out with your fingers, if you can. Nobody can lift a print off a slug."

"Well, that was bee's knees." The sheriff pulled himself from the trunk. He grinned as he displayed a mushroom shaped chunk of lead between his thumb and forefinger. "The thing nearly fell into my hand."

"At least I wasn't the one who had to poke around in there."

Doctor Whitlock grabbed the spent slug. "I'll check this out after I do the autopsy. If you want, come along with me. I could use your help. I can think of a couple of pretty nurses who'd be really grateful."

"Too busy," Sam said without hesitation. "There's only me and Burke to do all the work. You've forgotten the rest of the men are up above Wisdom, looking for the shell casing that slug came from."

"I suspect you'd best go back to your office and work on what we'll tell the bunch in Santa Fe. I'll give you a call when I'm finished. Come to the hospital, we'll go over my findings, then go to lunch."

Sheriff Sinrod sighed. "Don't hurry any more than you have to."

"I won't," the doctor said. "I surely won't."

Oliver Jordan placed the telephone receiver down onto its cradle. He stared for a moment out the front window at a cow elk that was nonchalantly walking down the deserted street.

"Who was it dear?" Harriet asked from the kitchen.

"That was Ronnie's wife, Minnie. She said the doctor called and Ronnie can come home tomorrow. That old Moon automobile of theirs is still not running. I told Ronnie he'd never be able to find parts for that car. She wants to know if we'd drive into Silver and pick him up. Minnie said if we would, she'd fill up our gas tank both ways."

"You told her we'd be happy to help?"

"Of course, Mama. I'm glad Ronnie wasn't hurt worse in that awful crash than just losing an eye. At least he can still see to pump gas."

Harriet came stomping in. Dishwater dripped from her hands. "Ronnie Bowdrie's blind in one eye!"

"Don't go getting worked up, Mama. It's not good for your heart. The good Lord only knows we've both been through enough lately. Minnie said the nerve in his right eye got cut in two by a piece of glass. There was nothing the doctors could do, but his other eye will heal up fine. Otherwise, he wasn't hurt much at all. It could have been a lot worse."

"That poor man who was burned to death when Ronnie's car wrecked, did Minnie say who he was? I take it he wasn't anybody from town."

"No Mama, she didn't mention anything except about Ronnie. I told her we'd have him home to her around five in the evening. This will give us time—"

"I don't suppose we can put it off."

"It's something that has to be done."

"Maybe Woody will be at his cabin. I think he'd like to come with us."

"We'll ask him, Mama, if he's there. If not, it'll be all right."

The frail old lady blinked away a tear, something she had become accustomed to doing. "You're right, Oliver. After tomorrow, things will be better. At least—" Harriet turned towards the kitchen. "At least we'll have kept our promise."

Doctor Whitlock took a testing sip of coffee from a mug that had been on his desk since early morning. He shuddered, set the coffee cup down and turned his attention to the sheriff.

"That slug you took from the back seat," the coroner said, "was from a thirty-thirty carbine such as a Winchester Model 94."

"How do we know this? I'm going to get grilled about these things right soon."

"Elementary, my dear Sinrod. Here in the United States calibers are based on hundredths of an inch in diameter. While all slugs become distorted when they strike objects, I was able to measure this one at thirty hundredths. From the fact that part of a blunt end of the bullet remained unscathed, along with the weight, I deduced it came from a thirty-thirty. In a carbine, the bullets are blunted on the ends to keep them from igniting the primer on the cartridge in front. Therefore, you are looking for the murder weapon I first described."

The sheriff's expression turned grim. "That's only the most popular deer rifle around. I'd guess every third man in Grant County has one." He hesitated. "Even that friend of Pat Gunn's, Woody Johnson, said he had one. The old fellow lives right near where the killing happened. I should go get that weapon. Did you find enough rifling groves on the slug to do a ballistics match?"

The coroner nodded. "All things considered, it's in fairly good shape. Bring in the rifle; I'll take it to Ludwig's slaughterhouse and fire it into a pig's head. That should approximate the damage. I'm betting this will clear Woody Johnson."

"He could've been thinking he was doing his friend a favor—shooting that arson investigator."

"No, you forget he was with the truck driver who drove Marshal Bowdrie to the hospital at the time of the shooting.

I just want to eliminate that Winchester of his to save him grief."

Sheriff Sinrod eyed the full cup of coffee. "You going to drink that?"

"Help yourself."

"I'll pass; from the look in your eye it's likely embalming fluid."

"No it isn't. Embalming fluid tastes a lot better, trust me on this."

The sheriff leaned forward in his chair and tented his fingers on the doctor's oak desk. "I understand Ronald Bowdrie's blind in one eye. That's a shame; any lawman being shot is a tragedy."

"Actually, he was very lucky. If that shard of glass had been traveling much faster, it would have penetrated his brain and killed him on the spot. Aside from a few cuts and bruises, he's fine. Doctor Cleary's releasing him tomorrow. They left his bad eye in its socket. He'll have to wear a patch, but most people adjust really well to having only one eye."

"I took a moment to visit with Bowdrie before coming here. The man's in a red rage to have Pat Gunn arrested. He claims that with him having only one eye, he can't be a state policeman. I've seldom seen anyone in such a state as Bowdrie's in. The man's out for Gunn's blood."

"I'll order him sedated and make sure he's sent home with a supply of strong medication that'll keep him quiet and rested. I think that'll do us all a lot of good."

"Let's go eat lunch, then start making our phone calls. Ellie's Diner has got meatloaf on special. It comes with mashed potatoes and gravy."

"Sounds great. Autopsies always spark my appetite."

"I'm terribly sorry I was too busy to help."

"I bet you are." It was the doctor's turn to become grim. "Sam, I put the officer's death down as due to a gunshot wound to the head. But there's more."

The sheriff raised an eyebrow. "Something else killed him?"

"No, the bullet did the trick. When I do an autopsy I always make a Y cut beginning at each shoulder to the bottom of the rib cage, down the belly and ending at the groin. I also used a trephine saw to cut away what remained of his skull. Then I took out all of the internal organs, weighed and examined them. Officer Keller had a tumor the size of a hen's egg at the base of his brain. My best guess is that he was suffering from splitting headaches and likely had some obvious changes in his behavior. He'd have died in a few weeks at most."

"I suppose a person could say his time was *really* up."

"Whoever shot that man saved him from a lot of pain. At least he died fast. Considering the circumstances, it was a blessing in disguise."

"The question is: did the shooter know that? Maybe I ought to make some inquires, such as whether or not there was a big life insurance policy issued on Frank Keller not too long ago. One of the things you said when we were in Wisdom was, 'This case would take some twists and turns.' "

"Check it out." The doctor stood, went to the door and grabbed his hat from a clotheshorse. "Well, we've beat our gums long enough. Ellie's meatloaf sells out in a hurry."

Sam Sinrod's appetite had fled, yet the prospect of lunch appealed to him more so than making phone calls to the capital. "Yeah," he said listlessly. "Let's go."

CHAPTER THIRTEEN

A ray of golden sunlight knifing underneath the drawn window shade added sparkling beauty to Pearl Dunbar's emerald eyes. She lay alongside Pat Gunn, naked as the air, and just as unashamed.

The past night had witnessed the culmination of weeks of building desires. The resulting crescendo of pent-up emotions becoming fulfilled had left them both spent.

The couple had just finished making love for the third time. Pat reached to the night stand, fished out two Lucky Strikes from a crumbled pack. He placed one between Pearl's ruby lips, mouthed the other, then lit both cigarettes with one match.

Pearl took a long drag on the Lucky, placed it into an ashtray and rolled to face Pat, brushing an unruly lock of scarlet hair from her eyes as he slid closer. "I've wondered for weeks how it would be to go to bed with you. Now I know; it's Heaven and I'm sorry only that we waited."

Pat sighed contentedly, reached over and teased a taut dusky nipple with his forefinger. "If this is Heaven, I'm going to have to change my ways, because I never want this to end. I'd hate to chance the Devil finding I'd slipped through his claws and come take me away from you."

Pearl gave a robust laugh. "The very thought of Lucifer snatching you and letting me go would give a hundred preachers apoplexy. I'm the type of woman every mother warns her son about."

"You're the real cat's pajamas, my sweet." Pat took a

puff of his Lucky and gave her a wicked wink. "Just being close to you would set off matches. Men have been chasing skirts since Adam chased Eve around the apple tree. If guys go to perdition for that sort of thing, I reckon the Devil's had to put sideboards on Hell to hold everyone."

"That's what I like about you Pat. A lawman has been killed and you're the prime suspect. The town has died around us, there's a world war raging and you can still smile. Not only that, but you're able to make me feel better about myself than I have a right to do."

"All we have to do is survive until the war's over. Things will be back to normal in jig time when that happens. Honestly, I don't have a clue who shot that poor arson investigator. All I know for sure is that it wasn't me, so there's absolutely no reason to be concerned over the matter."

Pearl swallowed, but sparks of anguish remained stuck in her throat. The world was cruel and filled with many real dangers that often ruined the innocent and trusting as easily as the evil and guilty. Sweet, wonderful Pat Gunn had every reason to despair, yet he seemed immune to the slings and arrows of misfortune. To cause gloom in this man would be akin to throwing acid on Santa Claus. She simply could not do it.

"Of course things will turn out fine," her mouth was dry and dusty as old parchment. "In a little while, everything will be jake again."

Pat snuffed out his cigarette. He turned on his side, gathering her snugly into his arms. She gave a soft moan as she raised to meet his oncoming lips. The kiss was long, velvety, soothing. It transported Pearl on a soft and wispy cloud to a place where there is only love, a land that can be visited but briefly. Memories of scant moments, however, can last and comfort for a lifetime.

* * * * *

"Dad-blast it," Woody Johnson swore, after banging his knuckles for the third time attempting to tighten the same joint of pipe. "God never meant for people to take baths indoors. Wallowing around in a great big tub of hot soapy water, plain and simple ain't a normal thing for a person to do."

But then, he reflected as the pain lessened, women weren't exactly normal. They did smell nice, which he thought agreeable. He also knew that to keep them smelling nice he had to put in a hot water system come hell or high water. Being on the side of a mountain, high water wasn't much of a worry. That only left the hell of plumbing for him to suffer through.

Woody had been working since sunrise, piping a rusty metal tank that he'd strapped crossways across the back two burners of his kerosene cookstove to the water line from the storage tank in the mine. The two rear burners were actually wasted space. A skillet and stew pot only took one front burner each and would cook enough food to fatten an army. Heating bath water would be the first good use the rear burners had ever been put to.

The gray-haired miner had always prided himself on being spic and span enough to pass muster. A number two washtub full of water set in the middle of the kitchen floor, a bar of lye soap, along with a bristle brush once in a while kept him in fine order. Then he would wash his clothes in the same water to be thrifty. Now, things in that department were definitely going to have to change.

At least the mine tapped a plentiful supply of good water. By piping it from an underground storage and letting it run a small stream continuously, the line never froze. Heating an entire thirty gallons of water would cost a lot of money, however. Kerosene was selling at the unheard of price of eight cents a gallon. Every time a woman took a bath it could easily cost as much as fifteen to twenty cents. Then a satisfied look crossed Woody's stubble-bearded face when he remembered the sweet aroma of spring cherry blossoms. Twenty cents every week would be money well spent.

He had fastened the Stillson wrench onto the pipe and gritted his teeth to prepare for another knuckle-bashing that was likely coming, when the distinctive, rhythmic chugging of an approaching Model A took his attention. Visiting with nearly anyone would be an improvement over losing more skin.

Woody left the wrench gripping the pipe, wiped his hands and went to see who had come calling. He really hoped it was Lonnie Dillman starting to haul away scrap iron. The sooner he got his hands on counting money, the sooner he could get on with his new goal in life. Then, he realized sadly, Dillman drove a big Reo truck, not a Model A.

When Woody came out on the porch, he saw Oliver and Harriet Jordan turning their battered station wagon around on what little flat ground there was, so it would face heading downhill when the engine was shut off. This was a smart thing to do in case the car refused to start. The mine and cabin were all uphill from the highway, allowing a vehicle to roll down and build sufficient speed to start, if it ever was going to, without the bother of cranking or towing.

"Howdy friends," Woody said as he strolled to open Harriet's door for her. "What brings you good folks up here on such a nice day?"

Oliver was out of the car and standing beside Woody before the frail Harriet had made it to her feet.

"Rheumatism, along with a bum ticker has her stove

up," Oliver said matter-of-factly. "Gets worse in the wintertime."

"I'm up to making the climb," Harriet said, her words seemed forced and hollow. She surveyed Woody with reddened eyes. "If what we're here for is all right with you, I can make it."

Oliver placed a hand on his friend's shoulder. "I need to explain. When you saw us the other day, we'd gone to Silver City to pick up Robert."

"Well, your son's come home. Thinking back on the matter, it's been some time since he went and joined the Army." Woody stepped to one side and looked inside the station wagon. "I surely wish you'd brought him along. I ain't seen little Bob for a coon's age. The last I'd heard, he's made sergeant first class. You two must be plenty proud—"

The miner's words stopped quick as if he had been punched in the mouth. Only being socked would not have been so painful as the harsh realization that struck when he saw the brass urn cradled in the crook of Harriet's arm and realized why she was dressed in black.

Oliver brushed a fist past a leaky eye. "The telegram said he was killed by a sniper in North Africa on the eighth of October. That's the same day the mines here were ordered closed. Our son and our town were both cut down on the same day.

"At times it's awfully hard to understand what God could have been thinking to allow anything like this to happen. A chaplain wrote us that the Almighty had need of Robert's soul. I'm of the mind he could have waited, at least until Mama and me were gone. Hell of a world where the parents have to bury their children."

"I'm terribly—" Woody hesitated. The word "sorry" was

vapid, meaningless. "I'm terrible hurt by this. I truly am. This blame war's being fought thousands of miles from here, yet it's gone and killed one of our own."

"When Robert was growing up here in Wisdom . . ." Harriet could have been reciting a recipe. All emotion had been long since wrung from her frail body. "Ronnie and he, along with most of the boys, liked to climb to the top of Angel's Roost Mountain. He said from up there a person can almost reach up and touch the face of God."

"When he went to war . . ." Oliver's voice was stronger now. "Robert wrote us if anything happened to him that he wanted to be cremated and his ashes scattered to the winds from that peak."

"I'd be obliged if you'd let me come along," Woody pointed to an opening in some trees. "The trail's in good shape. It'll only take but a little while for us to get there."

Harriet eyed a puffy white cloud passing overhead. "It's a good day for Robert to come home." She turned to her husband. "Isn't it dear?"

The old man said nothing. He simply nodded, wrapped a sheltering arm around his wife's shoulder and helped her begin their arduous trek.

"You two go on ahead," Woody shouted, heading for the door. "I'll catch up with you in just a bit. There's something I need to get."

A little more than an hour later the trio stood on the gray, barren, windswept peak of Angel's Roost Mountain. The ascent would have taken much longer if Harriet had not consented to allow Woody to carry her. The frail lady weighed nearly nothing, even cradling the brass urn in her arms. Every beat of her heart was so violent it shook her as if she were being jolted with electricity. Woody held no doubt she would have passed away before reaching the summit, had she not allowed his assistance.

"I can see why Robert loved this place so much." Harriet's wheezing voice filled with determination. "There's the whole town of Wisdom laid out below."

"And those mountains we can see way over to the west . . ." Oliver motioned with his head as he shouted to be heard above the moaning wind, "are in Arizona. Imagine being able to see that far."

"Does the wind always blow up here?" Harriet asked.

"Yes, Ma'am," Woody answered quickly. "All the years I spent on the side of this mountain, it's howled real regular. I reckon there ain't nothing to slow it down any, if a person gives the matter some thought."

"That's good. Robert always liked seeing new places. From here he can visit them all." Harriet held out the urn. "Take the lid off this, dear. It's time to bring our son home to where he wanted to be."

Woody stepped closer to the bereaved couple so he could be heard over the keening west wind. "It seems like just the other day that Bobbie and his friends would come laughing and playing by my place on their way up here. Nowadays, there's no kids and there's no laughter."

"War kills the both of them." Oliver laid a shaking hand on the lid of the urn. "I was hoping the last war might have taught the world a lesson, but it didn't."

Woody reached into the pocket of the tattered leather jacket he had put on for the walk. "If you folks don't have any objections"—he held up a harmonica—"I can play 'Amazing Grace' without making a botch of it. A person should always have a preacher or church music to help send them off."

"I think Mama and I'd like that," Oliver said as he gave

the brass lid a turn. "We'd like that a lot."

Woody made a couple of steps upwind, cupped his hands around the silver mouth harp and began playing. The melodious chords blended with moaning gusts of wind to be carried and bounced as echoes through the craggy canyons below.

Oliver Jordan removed the lid from the urn and placed it in his pocket. With the formality of a priest offering the sacrament, he reached out, grasped his wife's hand to the vessel, then without hesitation, upended it.

A thin wispy cloud of black snaked across the blue horizon before disappearing against the backdrop of gray and green mountains.

"We kept our promise, Mama," Oliver said, staring down at the town below. "Robert's home now."

"Yes dear," Harriet sobbed. "Our son's home to stay."

Spinner Olsson was shuffling his way along Midas Creek heading for his usual spot on a barstool at the Happy Eagle when an unusual sound caused him to stop, cock his head and look about.

After a long moment the old fellow gave a wheezing cough and resumed his uphill journey. For some reason he thought he had heard a boy laughing.

That was a silly thing to think, he chided himself. *Everyone knows there aren't any children left in Wisdom. Not these days. It was only the wind, nothing more.*

CHAPTER FOURTEEN

Doctor Bryce Whitlock leaned back in his swivel chair, laced his fingers together behind his head and regarded Sam Sinrod from across a cluttered oak desk. "I told Barth Thornton to go ahead and cremate Keller's remains. I may catch hell for that decision, but I feel I owe it to the officer's family to chalk up his death as being killed in the line of duty. This way they won't have to battle with any insurance company."

The sheriff kept a jaundiced gaze on some of the more interesting items floating in glass jars that were littering the doctor's desk top. "I'd say that was mighty nice of you. From what you've told me about him most likely acting strange from having that brain tumor, I would venture they've already had enough to suffer without adding to their pain any."

Sinrod noticed one of the jars staring back at him, with a single eyeball floating in clear liquid. When he studied closer, he saw a severed finger with a painted nail that had a thin gold wedding band still encircling it around the knuckle, keeping the eye company.

The coroner had observed his friend's interest. "This is one of the more fascinating cases to come my way. Unfortunately, a single finger and eye aren't enough to make an identification as to who got killed. Especially when the finger pad area where the print impression would be had been shaved off, most likely with a straight razor."

"A lady's finger and an eye's all that was found?"

"That's the size of it. Sheriff Mayes, down in Lordsburg, had a man who was fishing on the Gila bring him an eye that he'd found floating in the river. Victor Mayes didn't know if it was human or not, so he sent it to me. When I confirmed he had a person's eyeball, a search party was formed to comb the area. That single finger was all they found, and it was a mile upstream under a mesquite bush."

"So some lady got butchered and no one even knows who it was." The sheriff grinned slightly. "Well, you can always claim that you didn't have much to work with."

Whitlock snorted, unlaced his fingers and sat upright. "I'll solve that case. It will take me a while is all. People start talking or bragging after they feel enough time has passed. They get brave, drunk or stupid. Sometimes all three. Then we'll make the arrest. There's no statute of limitations on murder."

"At least we *do* know who our latest victim was," the sheriff said. "I worry just how much that will help us find out who shot him. None of my men were able to find a single thing when they scoured the area yesterday. Not a shell casing, empty beer bottle, or even cigarette butts to indicate where the killer might have waited.

"It's a fact he had to have been there for some time. No one could pin down when Bowdrie would have been driving Officer Keller into town to within two or three hours at best."

The coroner reached out and began nervously spinning the jar with an eye in it. "I think we had better drive to Wisdom right away. I want to bring in the Johnson fellow's rifle for testing. Then we'd better get statements from as many people as possible who might have seen anything."

"Let's go have breakfast. It's still early; we can be there by ten. If things go well, we can make it back here before the folks from Santa Fe start roaring in." Sinrod nodded at the twirling jar. "Maybe we'll get lucky and someone in Wisdom kept an eye out for what happened there."

Irene Chapman was alongside Midas Creek, picking what few green sprigs of wild mint that could be found after the ice storm of the other day. The harvest was a meager one, causing her to wonder if possibly drinking bourbon over hailstones, like Pat Gunn did, might be less bother than fussing with making juleps.

Then a sheriff's patrol car pulled up in front of the Starlight Theater and took her mind off picking mint, especially when she caught a glimpse of Woody Johnson riding in the back seat where they always carried handcuffed criminals.

It took only a brief moment for her to dump the apronload of mint into the sink. "Wake up, you old poop." Irene elbowed her husband as she scurried by. The old man had dozed off while listening to Glen Miller on the radio. "The cops have arrested Woody for murdering that arson investigator!"

Fred let out a yelp, blinked sleep from his eyes and went to see what his wife was ranting about. A stray kitten showing up was enough to cause that woman to burst an eardrum with her yelling.

"Woody got murdered?" Fred asked, still groggy from being painfully shaken from a relaxing nap.

"Well shucks," Irene said dejectedly from the open doorway. "He ain't handcuffed. From the looks of things, the two cops and Woody are just looking for Pat. I reckon it was a false alarm."

"You went and smashed my ribs to show me a sheriff's car?"

"They ain't gonna find Pat at the theater," Irene said, ignoring her husband. “He’s most likely up at the Happy Eagle with that hussy.”

“Pearl’s no hussy, dear, that’s your department. And I don’t blame Pat at all for getting his ashes hauled while he’s still young enough to remember why men put up with women.”

“Go back to listening to your radio, you old poop.” Irene craned her neck, surveying up and down the main street. Aside from the sheriff’s car not another vehicle or person could be seen. “I’m gonna fix me a julep. It’ll be afternoon shortly.”

Fred Chapman rubbed his ribs as he walked to the cooler and extracted a bottle of beer. “You do that, dear.” A thoughtful look crossed his stubble-bearded face. “And I’m glad Woody didn’t get himself murdered.”

“Jiggers!” Nero screeched when the door to the Happy Eagle swung open. “Bugger ’em, bugger ’em.”

Alvin Kent reached down and swung his dead legs around to face the newcomers. He was sitting on a stool at the bar, sipping a cup of tepid coffee. There were fewer and fewer reasons he could think of to play the piano, at least when the madam wasn’t in the reception area. His face registered only mild surprise when he saw that one of the three men coming inside sported a sheriff’s uniform.

“Good morning, gents,” Alvin said. “The bar’s not open yet. If you want a drink, though, I can yell for Carla.” He squinted at the sheriff. “She’s our regular bartender. I’d guess she’s in the back of the building right now, getting ready to open the place.”

“Howdy Alvin,” Woody said nonchalantly. “Don’t bother with any pleasantries. These men only want to talk to Pat. Is he about?”

A wry smile crossed the professor's young face. "Uh yeah, I think he came in a bit ago to visit with Pearl." He looked at Sam Sinrod. "Miss Dunbar owns this little bar."

"Calm yourself, fellow," Sam said. "Everyone from Santa Fe to Tucson knows this joint is a cathouse. I don't care about that in the least. I'm here on a homicide investigation." He nodded at the red-curtained doorway. "Could you go fetch the owner?"

Alvin reached for his crutches, which caused the sheriff's face to redden with embarrassment. The lawman silently chided himself for looking around for scantily clad ladies rather than noticing the young man was a cripple. But, he had heard a lot of really good stories about some of the girls who worked here.

"Hello, Woody, gentlemen." Pat Gunn parted the velvet curtain and stepped through the doorway buttoning his shirt. Gliding close behind came Pearl Dunbar dressed in a *very* revealing silky green nightgown that fit her lithe figure like a second skin. "What can we do to help you boys?"

Woody got something caught in his throat. He gave out a gurgling wheeze that would have done Spinner proud. Then he went and took a seat alongside Alvin without uttering a single word.

Doctor Whitlock stepped forward and introduced himself to Pearl. The sheriff had apparently caught the same malady that had struck Woody Johnson. A low mewing sound seemed to be the best the sheriff of Grant County could manage at the moment.

"Mister Gunn," the coroner said, reluctantly turning his attention from the beautiful redhead, "the man killed outside of town *was* a state arson investigator Marshal Bowdrie had called in to investigate your house fire."

Woody gave out a cough, then said to Sinrod, "Thanks

for calling and letting us know Slow Ron only got blinded in one eye. Things plumb looked a lot worse when we found him."

The sheriff tore his gaze from lusciously tempting cleavage. "Frank Keller was the man shot. He leaves a wife and kids. With him being a state lawman, there will be an investigation hit this town like no other ever has. Mister Gunn, I have to search your theater. The state boys may be satisfied if we do it. I promise we won't tear up your place like they will."

"I have no objection at all to your poking around the theater," Pat said. He lit a cigarette. "Ron Bowdrie clearly is trying to make a name for himself. I suffered an accidental fire, plain and simple. An innocent man has nothing to hide."

"We're merely investigators," Sam said. "Not a judge or a jury. Facts are all we're after."

Doctor Whitlock said to Pat, "I remember you saying that the owners of the Bloated Goat Saloon may have seen you. We'll want to question them while we're here, along with anyone else who may be able to verify your movements that afternoon."

"There's not many people left around here these days." Pat took a puff of his cigarette and blew a smoke ring. "Joe Godfrey and his wife still live in a log cabin behind their restaurant. Those poor folks' house suffered a misfortune from lightning earlier this year, come to think on the matter. They had a real nice home farther down Midas Creek. It burned clear to the ground and Slow Ron never thought a thing about it. I would say that man has it in for me."

"The best count I've got . . ." Pearl bathed the sheriff in a cloud of cherry blossoms as she brushed by him on her way to get a cup of coffee, "is about thirty people still living here. I'd say half of those or more have ranches or homes outside of Wisdom." She sighed sadly. "Hard to believe only a few months ago this town was booming with thousands of working miners living here in town."

"War is the science of destruction." The coroner lit a cigarette and continued. "A very smart preacher made that observation almost a hundred years ago. This worldwide destruction of civilization that we have going on will change the future forever. My greatest fear is that we'll be fighting on our own soil before much longer."

Pat waved his hand dismissively. "Nah, I've been reading about a secret weapon the government has. I'm betting in only a few months the war will be over and things will be back to normal. The mines here still have lots of gold. They'll reopen and folks'll move back here faster than they moved away."

The doctor took a moment to reply. His face betrayed no emotion when he spoke. "Millions and millions of innocent people, along with myself, hope with all of our hearts that you're right about that. For now, however, we need to get on with this homicide investigation."

Sam Sinrod had recovered from the shock Pearl had given him, but to be on the safe side, he kept his gaze away from her tempting figure. "Mister Gunn, get your shoes on. We need to search your place."

"The door isn't locked. You boys go on down and get started doing what you have to," Pat said with a shrug. "I'll be along in a bit."

Sinrod said, "I appreciate your understanding." He nodded at the coroner. In a moment they were gone.

"Bugger 'em!" Nero screeched, flapping his wings excitedly. "Get a poke. Bugger 'em!"

Pat glared at the parrot. "I hope you choke on a sunflower seed and cough your beak off." Then he turned and went in the backroom to retrieve his shoes.

"Well, it's a fact that no one in Wisdom can verify Pat Gunn's whereabouts when Keller got shot." The sheriff rolled up the window of his cruiser. The weather had turned biting cold. "I don't know if the old couple that owns the Bloated Goat are really certain what state they live in. Drinking during the day will kill them off sure as God made little green apples."

"They've had their lives turned upside down," Doctor Whitlock said. "People handle hardship differently. I would advise them to quit drinking, but they wouldn't listen."

"Can't say that I'd blame them any." The sheriff looked through the windshield at a pewter sky as snowflakes began to fall. "Anyone with good sense knows there's more old drunks than old doctors."

The coroner ignored the gibe. He reached over and turned on the heater. "If the snow doesn't get too deep, I'm going to come back here and spend a day going over the crime scene. We need to find that shell casing."

"My men gave the place a good going-over."

"I know they did, Sam. I'm not blaming anyone. The old miner's rifle we're bringing along will only prove it's not the murder weapon. Pat Gunn's place was clean as a whistle. We don't have clue one as to who killed that officer, and we'll be up to our hinders in state lawmen when we get back to Silver City. I'm at a loss to know what to tell them."

"It's a cinch Pat Gunn is innocent."

Doctor Whitlock cocked his head. "And how did you come to that brilliant conclusion?"

Sinrod grinned, keeping his eyes glued to the twisting

wet road. "Any man smart enough to charm the madam of a cathouse into dropping her drawers and come across with free nookie is certainly too smart to shoot an officer of the law." He hesitated. "Or at least get caught if he did."

Whitlock groaned and lit a fresh smoke. "Just drive," he said with a sigh. "And try to get us back to Silver City in pieces big enough to be chewed on by that bunch from the capital."

CHAPTER FIFTEEN

The huge red Cummins diesel truck towing a flatbed trailer groaned to a stop in front of the Bloated Goat Saloon. A moment later, Lonnie Dillman brought his battered Reo to a halt behind the Cummins.

In the growing shadows of approaching night, Fred Chapman stood, hands on his hips, watching with wonderment through the window at the end of the bar as four men clad in overalls climbed down from the trucks.

"Wake up, dear," Fred said, turning to shake his wife's shoulder. "We've got some honest to goodness paying customers headed our way."

Irene bolted upright with a snort. It took her a few seconds to clear her mind enough to recognize Lonnie as he and the others came through the door.

"Howdy, boys," she said hoarsely. "It's great to see some working men here in Wisdom again. Have a seat and name your poison."

"Snowing a mite up on Angel's Roost Pass," Lonnie said, hoisting himself up on a bar stool. "From the looks of things here, it doesn't appear it'll be much of a storm. That's good; my brother and cousins and me have a lot of work cut out for us."

Fred reached over the bar and shook the hands of Denny Dillman, along with Keenan and Rodney Sears, as they introduced themselves. All of the men had thick calluses from years of hard labor. It felt reassuring to have hardworking men in his saloon again.

"Give us all a bottle of beer," Lonnie said. "We can afford to spend a little money, as big as this job is. My best guess is we'll be employed here until next summer, at least."

Irene focused on the men while Fred went to the cooler to get the beers. "You fellows must be opening a mine. Did someone go and find a vein of lead or copper hereabouts? That'd be the best thing for this town. Bring in another boom, it would."

Lonnie Dillman sighed as he wrapped a ham-sized hand around the frosty bottle of Budweiser. "Folks, you'll find this bad news, but we start scrapping out the big Hidden Treasure Mine tomorrow. I've got a few days work left on the Mountain Lily and Woody Johnson's mine. Then the Hidden Treasure's all that'll be left up here worth bothering with."

Fred Chapman nearly spilled his beer; his heart skipped a few beats. "I don't think I heard right. Ira Tischler would never scrap out the Hidden Treasure. That mine was employing over five hundred men just a few months ago. The mill's not ten years old and it runs a thousand tons of ore every day."

Lonnie reached inside of his overalls and extracted a letter that he opened and handed to the bar owner.

"I got this by airmail," Lonnie said. "First letter I ever had that came by airplane that was also registered. You'll see where I'm authorized to remove any and everything of value from the property of Hidden Treasure Mines and sell it for whatever I can get. You can see it's signed by President Tischler, himself. It's the war effort that he's worried about."

Chapman's hand trembled as he read what he knew was an obituary for the town of Wisdom, along with their business.

"On the good side," Lonnie said, attempting to be cheerful. "We'll be spending money here for months to come."

"Then what?" Fred asked, his voice breaking.

Lonnie Dillman had no answer. The big man and his relatives drank in silence.

Irene studied the letter, folded it closed, handed it back to the scrap dealer, then stumbled off to fix herself another mint julep. Numbness, many times, is preferable to reality.

"We've been waiting here for hours," the gaunt, gray-haired man with a bushy moustache grumbled. His state police uniform was spotless, far too natty for a man who had driven a long distance.

Sheriff Sinrod nodded and offered a handshake to the man who had complained, along with another lawman, a portly, stern-faced Mexican. Both men were sitting across the sheriff's desk when the doctor and he had stepped inside the office.

The state lawmen's handshakes were brief, formal, indifferent.

Sam said in a conciliatory tone, "I'm Sheriff Sinrod and this is Doctor Whitlock. I'm sorry about the wait, but the coroner and I were investigating Officer Keller's homicide. Wisdom, as I'm sure you know, is some distance north of town."

The older man with dark, deep-seated, emotionless eyes who had first spoken to the sheriff said, "I'm Sergeant Garret Black. My supervisor here is Neto Diego. I'm sure you men know why we're here. Let's get to it."

"Gentlemen," Doctor Whitlock said happily, pumping first one officer's hand then the other. "How good of you to come to help us out. I can assume that you are the first of many rushing to our assistance from Santa Fe."

"You may call me Lieutenant Diego," the overweight officer with short black hair said curtly. "We are here, as you assumed, to bring justice to the murderer of one of our own. However, you are mistaken to think other lawmen will be coming. The sergeant and me are quite capable of handling this matter."

Garret Black stood. "We need copies of your reports to study. I also want the names of all of your suspects."

The coroner shot a glance at Black's gunbelt; then, before Sam Sinrod could answer, Doctor Whitlock interrupted, "The reports are not done yet. I'm afraid we don't have any suspects at this time. You men look tired. Why don't you go check into the Copper Mountain Hotel, it's a first rate place to stay. They also have an excellent restaurant and bar that I can recommend highly."

Neto Diego came to his feet with a grunt. "We expected to have those reports to read tonight. The sooner we get this—matter—resolved, the better it will be for *all* of us."

"My thoughts exactly," Doctor Whitlock was beaming. "A rested person is much more capable. The sheriff and I will work late tonight. You can expect our reports after breakfast in the morning. Then we can discuss the case and let you men lead. I am absolutely certain with your help, we'll solve this case in short order."

The lieutenant looked at Garret Black and nodded. "It is getting late and I am tired. We will do as you suggest." He glared at the sheriff. "Nine o'clock in the morning, we'll be here for the reports and briefing."

"Gentlemen," the coroner said, "I assure you that we'll be waiting here for you and give you our utmost assistance."

When the two state lawmen had gone and the door

closed behind then, Sam plopped into his swivel chair. "OK, Doc, what's up? I know you smell something. I have copies of the reports they wanted here in my desk. You added to them this morning, so you knew they could be handed over anytime."

"This is wrong. This is *very* wrong. That tall man with the fish-eye look might be wearing a police uniform, but he's a killer. That much I know for fact."

"All right, Watson, I'm listening."

"The bullets in his gunbelt gave him away. They were White Crosses. I've only read about them, but I sure know what they are when I see them. The only people who use them are professional killers."

Sheriff Sinrod's eyebrows drew together. "White Crosses?"

"Thirty-eight caliber flat-nose bullets. The slugs are cut with a hacksaw twice, like a cross. Then the grooves are filled with cyanide, and sealed with wax. A person gets shot in the foot with one of those, he might just as well have been hit square in the heart. They're dead in moments. There's no deadlier poison than cyanide."

Sam Sinrod gave a low whistle. "I should have known things were rotten in Denmark when only two lawmen showed up from Santa Fe. I expected a busload. But cold-blooded killers wearing police uniforms, I must admit, caught me on my dumb cluck side."

"There's more to this than meets the eye. I have a friend, Doctor Rogers, with the attorney general's office. He can be trusted. I'll give him a call at his home later tonight. It's obvious some very high officials want this matter swept under the bed, darn quick."

"And they're not going to be picky about who gets buried in the process." The sheriff clucked his tongue. "I'm going to arrest Pat Gunn on suspicion of murder. The first thing in the morning, I'll have him picked up and put in jail here. I believe he's innocent, but he'll be the handiest one to blame or kill when he draws down on Garret Black."

"Pat Gunn doesn't even own a firearm. We know that for a fact."

"Oh, he'll have a loaded pistol in his hand. Trust me on this. A lot of lawmen carry a 'throwdown' gun to make a shooting appear agreeable. I'm only bringing the picture-show owner in to save his life."

Doctor Whitlock cocked his head in thought. "I want to go back to Wisdom and check out the scene of the shooting. The way things are shaping up, I'd better get there early and let you take care of meeting with those fine folks from the capital. Tell them I had an emergency. I'll drive Pat Gunn back with me to save one of your officers a trip."

"You're just going to walk up to a suspect in a murder and ask him real nice to ride back to town with you, where he'll be arrested and thrown in jail."

"No," Whitlock said, chewing nervously on his lower lip. "Actually, I think I'll invite him to stay in my house for a while. A person in a jail cell is a sitting duck for a professional."

"So, we've gone from just not liking those nice state policemen to aiding and abetting a murder suspect." Sinrod gave an evil grin. "I like it."

"If I find out anything from Rogers, I'll give you a call."

As the doctor was on his way out a taunting voice said, "Have fun tomorrow with that homicidal maniac, y'hear."

CHAPTER SIXTEEN

The red gold of a New Mexico morning grew brilliant over jagged mountain peaks to the east. Among the towering summits, a few fluffy white clouds were sitting peacefully in the unusual windless calm, as if they had been floating peacefully along and gotten snagged.

In the valley town of Wisdom, shadows were losing their battle with daylight.

Alvin Kent smiled thinly out the window of his room in the Happy Eagle at what would be his last sunrise. The most difficult part of the task facing him was getting his useless legs that were wrapped with heavy steel braces into the chair without falling until he had the rope noose in place around his neck.

There was no choice. Polio had ruined his life years ago. He had been a fool not to do away with himself then. Now, the only job he could manage, a lowly piano player in a cathouse, had ended.

Last night four men who were to start demolishing the huge Hidden Treasure Mine for scrap had come in for drinks. Of everyone there, only foolish, optimistic Pat Gunn had claimed this was not the end of Wisdom and things would get back to normal soon. Out of earshot of Pat, Pearl had sadly told both Carla and he that she was closing the Happy Eagle and they had to leave within a week.

But a cripple who had to put steel cages around dead legs and shuffle about on crutches had no other place to go. There was no future, not for Alvin Kent. He was not cut from the same sturdy cloth as President Roosevelt. Last night he had played the piano with golden fingers for hours. One of the burly men had dropped a lone dime into his tip jar to reward his efforts.

Carla had fared no better. None of those cheapskates had even offered to buy her a drink, let alone take her to a room. Only old Woody had kept her company.

God, he thought. *I love that girl.*

But it could never be. No woman could ever love a cripple; his life had been over for a long, long time. It was now time to accept facts and end the torment.

Alvin grabbed onto the dangling noose that was firmly tied around a rafter and hoisted one useless leg into the chair. He glanced at the wallet and letter on the nightstand beside his bed. There wasn't much to say in a suicide note. Just a few lines to tell everyone goodbye. The leather wallet held two hundred dollars, his life savings. It wasn't much, he knew, but he had written plain instructions that the money was to be given to Carla.

Sweet, beautiful Carla, with smiling eyes and hair of spun gold. He hoped the cash would be enough to carry her far away from Wisdom.

The second leg came easier. Using his strong arms, Alvin stood straight and tall in the wobbly oak chair. A warm liquid feeling, as if he was being immersed in oil, coursed over his lanky body as he pulled the noose tight around his neck.

"I love you, Carla," Alvin Kent said hoarsely.

Then, with the last good use he would get from his wasted legs, he kicked the chair away.

Bryce Whitlock stood in the middle of the lonesome highway to Wisdom, holding a broomstick and squinting into the bright morning sun.

From black marks on the road, he deduced where he stood was about where Bowdrie's vehicle had been when the shot crashed through the windshield and ended Frank Keller's life. The shock most likely had caused the chubby marshal to jerk the steering wheel and hit the brakes, which caused the tire marks.

When the burned DeSoto had been in the impound yard with the dead officer inside, the coroner had cut the broomstick to the exact height where the bullet had struck the man's forehead. By marking the spot where the slug had been recovered from the back seat, it was a simple task to calculate the angle of travel, and thus backsight to where the bullet had come from.

Doctor Whitlock placed a Brunton transit atop the broomstick and set the bubble to read level at sixty-two degrees of elevation. Then, his eyes widened as he sighted through the peep hole.

"Well, no wonder they never found that shell casing," he commented, taking his gaze from the transit to focus on an ochre colored mine dump that was near the top of a shear cliff. "The bullet came from a lot higher than anyone had reason to suspect. And I'll bet that mine gave whoever the shooter was a nice cozy place to wait."

Whitlock placed the transit and broomstick in the trunk of his shiny black 1940 Cadillac, then began searching for a trail that would lead him to the mine. This took only a few minutes. From the amount of broken limbs and footprints along the trail, it had likely seen more traffic of late than the highway.

Halfway up the steep mountainside, the doctor's eyes began to blur. His legs felt rubbery and his throat cried for water.

"Damn diabetes," he swore as he sat down on a small

boulder, fished two sugar cubes from his pocket and popped them in his mouth. By the time Whitlock lit a second Chesterfield, his strength had returned, allowing him to continue the arduous climb.

"Well now, here's something I didn't expect." The coroner stepped just inside the black maw of the mine tunnel. Using a handkerchief he grabbed a Winchester Model 94 rifle that leaned against the wall.

Taking the firearm into the light of day, he examined it minutely. He noted the caliber was a thirty-thirty, which verified his earlier findings. The doctor laid the rifle down, took a vial of fingerprint powder from his pocket and began brushing the Winchester from stock to tip of the barrel.

"At least this fits," he mumbled. Not a trace of fingerprints could be found. "Only an idiot wouldn't wipe a murder weapon clean. I'm betting they didn't think about the shells inside, however."

He picked up the rifle and gently jacked the lever enough to see the spent shell had not been ejected. A dusting of black powder showed clear prints on the brass casing.

"Gotcha," the coroner gloated. Feeling much better now that he was confident he had a fingerprint there was a spring to his step as he carried the Winchester down the steep trail on his way to visit Pat Gunn.

The fact that the murder weapon had been wiped clean, then "dropped" at the scene spoke of a professional killer's tactics. But why would a hit man overlook wiping the prints from the shells? He was certain now that there was far more to this case than anyone had first thought. Now, a state lawman with cold, hit-man eyes had come to put *somebody* in a grave and stop any investigation.

But why? What had Frank Keller been involved in to cause anyone to want his death swept quickly under a rug?

Whatever it was, it must reach to the highest levels of the state government. It definitely stank to high heaven.

Perhaps, he mused, as he placed the rifle into the truck, his physician friend who worked with the attorney general would know something helpful. Last night Doctor Rogers' wife had told him her husband was in Denver attending a conference, but that he should be home tomorrow and she would have him phone.

Doctor Whitlock clucked his tongue, slid beneath the steering wheel of his beloved Cadillac, started the V-16 engine that purred sweetly in his ears and headed for Wisdom to try and stop another killing.

CHAPTER SEVENTEEN

Neto Diego poured himself a steaming cup of coffee from a thick crystal carafe. Using silver tongs, he added one lump of sugar, then carefully measured a level teaspoonful of cream, which he stirred in quite slowly. Room service was a benefit he seldom had a chance to enjoy. In this instance, however, no one would question any expense. Not savoring every possible moment of extravagance would be such a waste.

"Shitkicking town," Garret Black commented from the couch where he sat cleaning his revolver. "I'm surprised they have a decent hotel. I'll be glad to get this job over with."

"Patience, sergeant," Diego said calmly. "You know what our orders are. You can use one of those poison bullets you are so proud of when I tell you. Until then, *do* attempt to be pleasant to the local officials. Attracting any more attention than necessary to the matter of Keller could bring us problems. *Severe* problems."

"Don't worry, I won't do anything that'll embarrass our esteemed attorney general."

Diego glared at his companion. Of all the lawmen employed by the state, he despised Garret Black most of all. The man was vicious. He also loved killing. Only the fact that he was stupid, along with being faithful as a pet dog, had kept him out of the electric chair. Dogs, however needed to be kept on a short leash and disciplined regularly to be useful.

"Sergeant Black," Diego's voice was cold as a December wind. "If you mention the name of Jack Sutton, or the office of attorney general even once again, I *will* shoot you myself."

"Yeah," Garret Black grumbled. He gave a curt nod, then returned to oiling his Smith and Wesson for the task to come. The surly Mexican he would bring down at a more opportune time. Patience was a difficult virtue, but it had its rewards.

Black smiled like a cat staring at a canary in a cage when he thought of shooting Diego. He vowed he would do this, right after he had killed the man called Pat Gunn.

"Morning Doctor," Pat Gunn said, standing beside the highway, gazing at the flashing theater marquee. Pat was so engrossed in thought that it never occurred to him to wonder why the coroner had pulled to a stop and climbed from his sleek car.

Pat placed a fist to his cheek, keeping his eyes on the sign. "I think I might have spelled the word 'break' wrong. The title just doesn't look right to me for some reason."

"Sucker," Whitlock said, causing the theater owner to give him his full attention. "You left out the 'c' in sucker."

"Oh yeah," Pat turned and squinted at the marquee. "I reckon I did leave it out at that." He sighed. "I can't see any reason to risk a busted leg to correct it, since I don't have the movie to show anyway."

"We need to talk." The doctor looked about, seeing no one. "I suppose here is as good of a place as any. Actually, I'd thought you'd be at the Happy Eagle."

"Pearl's a good friend, but she had a crowd of customers last night so I came home early. There's a bunch of men starting to scrap out the worn-out old machinery at the

Hidden Treasure to make way for all new stuff when they reopen the mine."

"I'm sure that won't be much longer." Whitlock's tone was one he reserved for patients who did not have long to live. "But I'm more concerned about the here and now, along with your safety."

"My safety? Why in the world would anyone want to do *me* harm? I'm just the owner of a theater."

"And a murder suspect." The doctor tapped a Chesterfield from a full pack and lit it. "This case has turned dangerous. The man who was killed on that mountain was done away with for reasons other than the fact he was coming to investigate your house fire."

"I never shot anyone."

"That, I don't question. But, you must realize you're the only person around with a reason to have had Officer Keller turn up dead."

Pat snorted. "I'm innocent. That man could've poked through the ashes of my house until the cows come home and I wouldn't have cared. Actually, I wish he had. Then I would be able to collect my insurance money."

"You don't understand, Mister Gunn. If you turn up dead for *any* reason, it would be a simple matter to declare you the murderer. The whole incident would then quietly go away."

Pat held out his hands, palms up. "I suppose I'm in the sheltering hands of the law."

"Right at this time, I don't think that's wise. The sheriff wants to put you in jail for your own protection. I came with an offer to drive you back to my home in Silver City; I have an extra bedroom. You'll be safe staying there with me until we unwind some loose ends."

"There's a lot you're not telling me."

"That's true, Mister Gunn. But I can say the same thing about you. I suppose, before I give you shelter under my roof, it would be wise to inquire as to why you spent time in prison?"

A slump came to Pat's shoulders. Then he surveyed the jagged snow-capped peaks for a long moment. "How did you know?"

The Coroner smiled. "I'm a doctor. I know everything. Actually, the fact that you live in a remote area and own no firearms aroused my suspicions. The whiteness of the skin around your eyes confirmed it. In prison, a person has to sleep with the lights on. A rolled up towel laid across your eyes, makes it dark, but also leaves a definite pallor. I would also surmise old habits are hard to break, otherwise you would not still have the giveaway lack of skin tone."

Pat swallowed hard, then fixed the doctor in his gaze. "Times were hard in the Depression, but I won't make excuses. I spent six years in stir for violation of the Volstead Act."

"You were a bootlegger."

"Actually, I, along with some friends, made a good living hijacking Al Capone's liquor shipments and selling the booze ourselves."

Doctor Whitlock arched an eyebrow. "From what I know of Capone, you're lucky to be alive."

"Scarface often found it cheaper and more efficient to have the law take care of his business problems. He had us set up with a shipment of Canadian whiskey that came so easy, we should have been suspicious, but weren't—until we came to the police roadblock a mile down the road. I was afraid something like this would happen. I'd been stashing cash in coffee cans and burying them where they wouldn't be hard to find."

"So that was why you spent time in prison." The doctor sighed. "Prohibition made criminals out of a lot of people who would not normally have broken the law."

Pat Gunn gave a hollow chuckle. "When I got out, what I'd been sentenced to prison for wasn't even against the law anymore. Rather ironic, don't you think. Anyway, I rounded up my money, bought a new Studebaker, then headed west. I wanted someplace to start over, someplace where no one knew of my past."

"So you wound up here in Wisdom, New Mexico." Whitlock looked to the lonely Starlight Theater and the marquee lights that flashed day and night. Then he rolled his gaze around the lifeless town. "Pack enough clothes for several days." The doctor's voice was soft. "And as to what we just talked about, well, I don't see any reason for any of that to come out. We'll keep it just between the two of us."

"Thanks, Doc." Pat breathed a sigh of relief. "I owe you one. I'll pack and go stay with you, if you believe it's wise."

"My gut feeling is that in a few days or so, I'll be weighing your liver on a scale if you don't."

"I'm packing already." Pat turned to the coroner with pleading eyes. "I sure would like to drop by Pearl's and maybe tell her I'm going fishing for a few days."

"That will work. I'll drive you up there, but don't mention a single word about going to Silver City or staying with me. Telling her you're taking a fishing trip to somewhere on the Gila River will keep everyone safe. The only reason I'm in town is to look over the scene where the shooting occurred."

"You're a swell guy, Doc."

"I know, I've been one for years." He tossed the butt of his cigarette onto the dry gravel and ground it out with the heel of his shoe. "Now, let's get a move on. I get nervous having a murderer about."

Pat said over his shoulder as he strode to the theater, "If you're waiting on me, you're wasting time."

"We found him only about a half-hour ago." Pearl Dunbar's voice was raspy and her hand trembled slightly as he pulled back the white sheet. The gray visage of Alvin Kent in death lay on a twin bed, eyes wide, purple tongue protruding through swollen lips. Strangulation is not an easy way to die.

"I ran to the kitchen, grabbed a butcher knife and cut him down," Pearl stammered. "There was no breath, no pulse. I carried him to his bed—he isn't very heavy, you know—then I woke Carla and called the sheriff. He told me you were in town and for me to go look for your car, a big black Cadillac. I was shook real bad by this—Alvin was a good kid. I'd have been out in a bit, I just was too upset to drive."

"Calm down, Ma'am," the coroner said. "There's nothing you could've done different that would have changed a thing."

Carla Holland sat on a chair daubing her eyes and sobbing at what was obviously a letter. "That sweet boy, never let on he would do this."

"Is that letter a note Alvin left us?" Pat Gunn's tone was soft as a breeze rustling aspen leaves. "If it is, you'd best hand it over to the Doc."

Carla sniffed and passed the letter to the coroner when he stepped close. "The ones who never talk about doing away with themselves," Whitlock said after a few moments, "are the ones who get the job done. From all that's gone wrong in Kent's short life, I can understand." He turned to the madam. "If I can use your phone, I'll call the sheriff and tell him to send out Barth Thornton and the hearse.

There's nothing to do now but the burying."

Pearl said, "Sure, it's up front in the parlor."

Carla daubed again at her eyes with a handkerchief. "Alvin didn't have any family that I know of. What'll become of him?"

The coroner drew the sheet over the corpse. He winced when he realized his thoughts had turned to Kent's leg braces and a penniless polio-ravaged young girl whom they might fit. "Don't worry about it. The county will pay for a wood casket and digging the hole."

Tears streaked Carla's cheeks. In the still-red glow of morning, they glistened like frozen moonbeams. "He won't even have a headstone. I'd say everyone ought to have a marker, so's folks will know who's buried there."

Pat said, "I can see to it that he gets a board with his name on it."

"That ain't right." Carla stood, a look of determination taking the place of sorrow. "I knew the boy was sweet on me. A girl knows that sort of thing. Alvin said in his letter he was leaving me the two hundred dollars in his wallet." She turned to the coroner. "Is the money mine?"

Whitlock stiffened. Then he reminded himself of the young woman's profession. "That isn't an issue. Alvin Kent's death was by his own hand. His instructions dealing with his estate were plainly written down. Yes, Ma'am, the money's yours to do with as you please."

Carla stepped to the nightstand, picked up the wallet and began counting the bills; they were mostly fives and tens.

"I count two hundred and three dollars," Carla said firmly. "Doctor Whitlock, what does a marble headstone cost?"

A burning lump grew in the doctor's throat. His groundless rush to judgment stabbed at his heart. "Uh, Ma'am, I'm not really sure, but I know for a fact a hundred dollars will get him a nice tombstone."

Carla peeled off the money and handed it to the coroner with a firm hand. "If you would please take care of buying it? I don't get out much."

"I'll see to it," the doctor said.

Pat Gunn and Bryce Whitlock drove past Bowdrie's gas station on their way to tell Woody that Carla had asked for him to come. Not a single word had passed between them since leaving the Happy Eagle.

"Even a small marble headstone costs two hundred dollars," Pat said.

"I know that." The doctor lit a cigarette and refused to talk anymore about the matter.

CHAPTER EIGHTEEN

Spinner Olsson's silver dollar pealed time and again on the bar. It was like the tolling of a funeral bell. Flipping and twirling, the coin broke the stony silence and made the waiting easier.

Normally, Spinner would have been thankful for the ride Woody gave him to the Happy Eagle. Alvin Kent's playing of the piano always cheered his spirits. Now he sat in gloom with his friends, awaiting the hearse to arrive from Silver City to take the body of the piano player from this dying little town.

Yet another distant boom echoed down the still valley. In this rare day of no wind, noise of the blast from Lonnie Dillman's crew blowing up machinery hung in the still air as long and heavy as rifle shots from a firing squad.

"This is a terrible thing," Carla said, regarding Woody across a small table with moist, red rimmed blue eyes. "I don't know what caused him to hang himself."

"Poor Alvin just got tired, most likely." Woody chewed on his lower lip. "I suppose a preacher might be able to tell us the why, but for me, I can only be sorry the boy's gone."

The crunching of tires on gravel outside announced the arrival of Barth Thornton's somber black hearse, which stayed Carla's reply.

"Would you like to take a drive with me for a spell?" Woody asked. "It's a mighty pleasant day out; we don't get many this nice up here."

Carla dried her eyes with a handkerchief. A vestige of a

smile returned. "I'd like that, Woody. I haven't been out near enough lately. Let me get my purse and a wrap."

The undertaker met Woody and Carla as they came out the door of the Happy Eagle.

"Good day to you folks," Barth said. He was a rigid six feet tall with slicked back gray hair, dressed in a worn black suit and wearing thick glasses. The man would have been right at home on the cover of *Funeral Director* magazine. "Is this where I might find the deceased?"

"Alvin Kent is his name, sir," Carla sobbed, then climbed quickly onto the seat of the battered Model A truck.

"A bereaved relative," Barth commented. "Such a sad sight."

Woody started to reply when another explosion from the Hidden Treasure Mine resounded off the towering peaks. The miner simply nodded, and took the driver's seat alongside Carla. In a moment, they were gone.

"What both puzzles and disturbs me," Sheriff Sinrod said to Doctor Whitlock, "is the fact that not an eyebrow was raised when I told those state boys Pat Gunn is our only suspect in Keller's murder. It's as if they'd already known that tidbit."

"Those two are more sinister than Professor Moriarty, my dear Sherlock. It is an obvious fact that Diego and Black are officers of the state. It's also a fact that I wouldn't turn my back on either one of them unless I was wearing armor. Thick armor."

"They ask questions—demand information from us—yet, give us nothing in return."

"Which is one of the reasons for us not to doubt them being genuine government employees. J. Edgar Hoover's close-lipped tactics are as catching among government workers as the common cold."

Sheriff Sinrod leaned back in his chair. "Then, my dear Doctor Watson, I suggest we concentrate our efforts on what is *not* obvious."

"I agree." Whitlock cocked his head in thought. "Pat Gunn is safe in my home. The story we put out is that he has gone fishing on the Gila with friends. This covers why his car is still in Wisdom. We both know that flashy Studebaker he drives stands out like a boil on a whore's nose. We have time to do some serious investigation in the matter of Officer Keller's murder without, hopefully, having anyone else killed."

"You said you found the murder weapon in a cave?"

"Actually, it was just inside a mine tunnel that was far higher on the mountain than anyone would have guessed."

"Now, we need to check it for fingerprints."

Doctor Whitlock sighed. "The rifle had been wiped clean on the outside. This is usually an indication of a professional hit. I'm hoping the shells inside will give us identifiable prints; they didn't appear to have been removed."

"If we get lucky enough to lift good prints, we'll have to send them to Santa Fe for comparison."

"I've given that matter some thought. Your office keeps files of locals who have been fingerprinted. I suggest that I do a comparison with what we have on file. If I come up empty-handed, then we can send them on to the capital."

"I agree," Sheriff Sinrod said. "In the meanwhile, I'll keep feeding bits of information to Diego and Black; maybe it'll be enough to keep them occupied. From what I gleaned by calling the desk at the hotel and requesting their bill, those two are *really* enjoying themselves here in Silver City."

"If they're having fun, they aren't out killing someone."

Sam Sinrod's expression turned somber. "That was too bad about the young fellow hanging himself in the cathouse. I heard he was a good piano player."

"Being the professor in a whorehouse was what I always wanted to do." Whitlock sighed sadly and lit a cigarette. "But my mother made me settle for being a doctor."

"I've got to get going." The sheriff came to his feet; he appeared tired. "A rancher has a rabid dog locked in his barn; old widow Morganstern is simply certain there is a prowler in her closet, again. To top off all of these great jobs, I get to take the two stooges from Santa Fe out to dinner tonight."

"I'm glad at least one of us is having fun, but things are looking up. Before I make rounds at the hospital and get my hands messy trying to lift fingerprints from shells, I'm going to go shoot a cute little piggy square in its head."

The doctor gave an evil grin, stood and turned. On his way out the door, Whitlock said over his shoulder, "Let's meet at Ellie's Diner for breakfast, about seven. We can have ham and eggs."

CHAPTER NINETEEN

"This here is where they buried Sergeant James Cooney," Woody said to Carla, pointing to a massive granite boulder that was bigger than a house. "He's the man who discovered gold hereabouts and caused the town of Wisdom to get built."

"Look at that," she said, running over to check out a concreted-over doorway into the tomb. "Someone hollowed out a mausoleum for him."

Woody jacked up one side of his jaw. The miner wasn't at all sure what a "mausoleum" was, but did not want to appear addle-brained in front of the lovely lady. At least Carla seemed to be enjoying herself. Driving as far as he had, burning expensive gasoline that was soon going to be rationed to four gallons a week, was not wise, but the girl needed cheering.

Briefly, Woody had worried if taking her to see a grave would be uplifting, considering the way her day had gone. Carla, however, seemed to be enjoying herself. In the area around Wisdom, there were not a lot of sights to see other than mines or a cemetery.

"Apaches killed him." Woody decided to avoid any reference to potentially embarrassing big words that he did not understand. "It was Chief Victorio and a bunch of his braves. They were more than a tad upset about having miners hacking away at the mountains."

Carla bent to inspect the inscription on the entranceway. "April 29th, 1880. Why, that was only sixty-two years ago.

A lot can happen in a short span of time." She turned to Woody. "Can't it?"

"I don't know for certain, I wasn't around then. I'll only turn fifty-nine my next birthday."

Carla smiled sweetly. She felt comfortable being with Woody Johnson. She found his innocence, along with his often-unplanned wit, to be refreshing. Especially when compared to the countless loudmouthed men she had endured for years.

"Why did they go to all that work of digging into such a large rock for a grave? I thought a wood casket was what they used in those days."

"That didn't work out." Woody came to Carla's side. He bathed in the heady aroma of spring cherry blossoms as he continued. "They gave Cooney a regular burying, but the Apache came back and dug him up. Those Indians were really pis—upset with him. Those redskins chopped up his body real bad. The sergeant was well liked, so his brother and a bunch of friends blasted out that hole in the rock. Then they cemented his remains inside. I ain't never figured out how they got that cement up here. But at least ol' Cooney's stayed put ever since."

"You know," Carla's voice was soft, wistful. "I would like more than anything to stay in one place, have a home of my own. It seems like I've been leaving one town for another all of my life. Now, I have to move on, but for the first time, I don't want to leave. And I don't have any idea where I would go if I did. Old whores aren't wanted anywhere."

"Please, dear," Woody turned Carla to face him and drew her into a sheltering embrace, "don't ever say that about yourself again. You're beautiful as a mountain flower and a right nice lady, to boot."

Carla stifled a sob. "You're a sweet, wonderful man,

Woody Johnson, but I can't remain in Wisdom. Pearl's closing the Happy Eagle and I have to move on."

"Why, I reckon I didn't know about Pearl's gonna close."

"She said she was going to tell folks tonight."

Woody said, "Then what I've been planning won't bear a wait."

The gray-haired miner dropped to one knee as he gently grasped Carla's right hand between both of his. Woody's voice trembled as he looked up at moist, blue, startled eyes. "I was going to wait until I had a genuine bathtub in my cabin before I asked you to marry me. But if you'll have me, I promise I'll buy you one and hook it up right soon."

Carla's lower lip quivered violently. She tried to speak, but the words would not come.

"I know I ain't got much to offer such a pretty young girl like you." Woody interpreted Carla's silence as a possible rejection. He had to do better with his proposal. "My truck needs a set of brakes in the worst way. And we all know there's no gold in my gold mine, but there will be once I sort the spooks out of my doodlebug. I can truthfully say I never told any other girl I loved her. But I promise you that I do love you, and I'll do my darndest to make you happy."

Carla gave a heartrending sob, which caused Woody to believe all was lost. Then, using strength the miner never suspected any woman capable of, she jerked him to his feet and wrapped tender arms about his neck. Carla kissed him full on the lips for what seemed like an eternity.

"Will you have me?" Woody asked once he gained enough breath to speak. He still wasn't certain from which direction the wind was blowing.

"I want you more than anything in this whole world," Carla said happily. "I'll be proud to be your wife." She asked softly, "Could we have a real wedding with a preacher and all? I don't want anything fancy, just to have the words said over us."

"I've got a gold wedding band in my cabin. It was my mother's, rest her soul. I'd be right proud to put it on your finger in front of any variety of sky pilot you fancy." He smiled down at the most beautiful teary face he had ever seen and added, "My darling."

The couple sat on a log by the creek in front of James C. Cooney's tomb, kissing and making plans until the chill and shadows of approaching dark caused them to depart.

"I'm sure sorry I couldn't join your dinner party last night." Doctor Whitlock sliced a huge bite of ham and looked at it with obvious glee. "I'm betting those two boys from the capital were more fun than a barrel of monkeys."

"Now that you mention apes and such," Sheriff Sinrod said, looking around to make sure they would not be overheard, "remind me to burn Darwin's book. The thing's a crock and gives furry animals a bad rap. Garret Black and Neto Diego are living proof there's no such thing as evolution."

"Tut-tut, Sherlock. Did 'ems have a rough evening?"

Sinrod sighed and ate a slice of toast with apple butter before he felt up to the task. "Sergeant Black ordered a dozen raw eggs. It seems that at one time most of his stomach got blown away by a shotgun blast. The man actually lives on raw eggs. He broke one at a time into a glass, added salt, pepper, or sometimes hot sauce. What's worse, he grinned like an idiot when he savored every disgusting gulp."

The coroner shrugged. "He was a cheap date."

"Not Diego. That man has to have a hollow leg. He

knew any expense account bill for two wouldn't be given a second thought. He ordered two T-bone steak dinners, the big one-pounders, rare. Then the man scarfed those, along with baked potatoes with sour cream, butter, peas, green beans and a loaf of bread. He drank two bottles of wine, then ate two banana splits for dessert. All the while Black slurped on those awful raw eggs. It was a *memorable* occasion."

"After I killed the little piggy and recovered the bullet, my secretary told me I'd had a call from Jim Rogers; he's the friend I mentioned, who works for the attorney general."

Sam Sinrod decided to eat while he listened. Last night he had barely touched his dinner and felt famished. He simply nodded for the coroner to continue.

"Doctor Rogers has a private practice of his own. He merely acts as a medical examiner when asked. One thing he is, however, is an excellent observer and listener. He knew all about your dinner guests. Diego and Black work for a special branch controlled by Attorney General Jack Sutton. The folks in the capital call them 'the janitors' because they're sent out to clean up messes.

"It's not well hidden that those two are nothing but hired killers with a license. We suspected this much. What we did *not* expect was this."

The sheriff laid down a forkful of golden hash browns. "And what, Watson, might that be?"

Whitlock decided all of the truth wasn't necessary. "Pat Gunn used to live in Chicago back in the twenties. He made enough money to buy that theater in Wisdom, along with his flashy Studebaker, by hijacking booze shipments off Al Capone."

Sinrod gave a low whistle. "I'm surprised Pat Gunn's

not pushing up several generations of daisies. Scarface isn't known for his forgiving nature." He lowered an eyebrow. "Isn't Capone out of prison and living in Florida these days?"

"Palm Island, Florida, to be exact. It's also a fact that he's suffering from tertiary syphilis, too. That disease attacks a person's mind in strange ways. Capone supposedly has millions of dollars hidden in foreign bank accounts that the F.B.I. never found. He's rich, powerful and sick. That's a bad combination if he was to remember an old wound and want to settle a score before it's too late."

"Yeah, I can see that." The sheriff returned to his breakfast. "But there's no way Al Capone had an arson investigator killed just to set up Pat Gunn as the murderer."

"Ah, but the game is afoot, my dear Sherlock. What I *did* find out from my esteemed colleague was that Jack Sutton came to Santa Fe from Chicago, where he was a well-known attorney. He also became quite wealthy by defending one very special client; Alphonse Capone."

The sheriff's forkful of hash browns froze at his lips. "Oh shit."

"My sentiments exactly," the coroner said, returning his attention to a rapidly cooling plate of ham and eggs.

CHAPTER TWENTY

Neto Diego turned his gaze from the license plate on Pat Gunn's Studebaker Eight to study an open notebook on the seat beside him. "That fancy damn car belongs to our mark, all right. Son of a bitch picked a convenient time to go fishing. *Too* damn convenient in my book."

Garret Black puffed on a thick Cuban cigar while running his hands around the steering wheel of the 1937 Packard Eight. He loved to drive this car. It had a silky smooth one-hundred-fifty-horsepower engine that would likely do a hundred miles an hour, if Diego would only let him try. The fat lieutenant always yelled at him to slow down every time the speed got interesting.

Sergeant Black also loved the Packard's spacious trunk. Aside from ample room for a body, it held two fully automatic Thompson submachine guns with hundred-round magazines and ten thousand rounds of ammunition. Assorted bottles of various poisons, knives, ropes, garrotes, a case of dynamite, leg irons and a few sets of handcuffs rounded out the items that were essential to their particular line of work.

"Fishing trips don't last very long," Garret ventured.

"Our orders were to get this job done quick. Pat Gunn shot and killed Frank Keller, an officer of the law. Then Mister Gunn pulls that thirty-eight pistol we have there in the glove box on us, and we shoot him. Neat and tidy, just like it should be."

"Only the damn mark ain't here." Black puffed furiously

on his cigar. "I really want to kill him soon and get out of this shitkicking place."

"I've always wondered," Neto grinned evilly at his partner. "You hate everyplace we go. Is there somewhere we could go kill a mark, and not have to listen to you bellyache all of the time?"

Garret Black turned to Neto, his face a mask of unrestrained fury. "That woman in Texas took me by surprise when she shot out my belly. I don't appreciate you making fun of that."

"A bad choice of words, I apologize. Texas is a tough place. It's easy for anyone to get shot in Texas." Neto thought for a moment. "But you *did* kill her husband."

Garret's face took on a satisfied look. "Yeah, I suppose I should've expected her to be upset with me. If I hadn't been such a trusting soul, I wouldn't be living on raw eggs. It plain don't pay to trust nobody these days."

"The correct use of words would be, 'it doesn't pay to trust anybody,' " Diego admonished. "Remember, we represent the best the state of New Mexico has to offer. It is very important that we use correct English at all times."

Someday, I'm going to kill that fat, steak-chomping idiot, Garret thought. *Cyanide would work perfect. The stuff is white, like salt. I'll set out a shaker full of it in a restaurant when he's not looking. Then I'll enjoy watching him fall face first into his entree.*

"Yes, sir," Garret said. "I'll remember."

"I suggest while we're in this miserable place, that it might be a good idea to ask around as to when Mister Gunn is expected to return. The lights are on at his theater, so I would not suppose he'll be gone long."

Sergeant Black craned his neck up and down the deserted streets of Wisdom. "Ask who, Lieutenant?"

"There is a marshal in town." Neto thumbed through his notebook. "Ah, here it is. A Ronald Bowdrie. He was driving the car when Keller got the top of his head blown off, lost an eye himself from flying glass. If anybody should want to help us find Pat Gunn, it'll be Bowdrie."

"That bar, The Bloated Goat, looks like it might open later. We could go knock on the—"

An old man came shuffling from a clump of fat spruce trees and onto the dirt road, taking Garret's full attention.

Neto Diego had rolled down the window on his side of the car to let out some of Black's awful cigar smoke. He poked his head into the clean, cool air. "I say there, sir. We're state police looking for a person who lives here by the name of Pat Gunn. Do you happen to know when he'll return?"

Spinner Olsson gave a cough and stepped over to the long Packard. "Why do you want to see him?"

"Official police business." Neto's reply was more curt than he'd planned.

"Never heard of him," Spinner wheezed. "And I've been here for years."

Neto took a deep breath, reached into his pocket and drew out a dollar bill. "*Now* do you remember Pat Gunn?"

Spinner snorted. "George Washington's got a bad memory. Abe Lincoln, now there's a face that brings things into focus."

Diego's eyes narrowed as he fished out a five-dollar bill and handed it to the old man. "When will Mister Gunn be back in town?"

Spinner tucked the bill into his overalls with a shrug. "Hard to say, he went fishing, you know. Could be a day, could be a month. The moving picture theater's been closed for weeks." He turned to walk away.

"Then perhaps you could at least point out Marshal Bowdrie's home." Neto's voice was raw and cold as a north wind.

"Sure," Spinner said. "Him an' his wife own that gas station right over there about three hundred feet." His bearded face turned up in a grin when he pointed to the Standard Oil sign. "Y'all have a nice day now, y'hear."

"Shitkickers," Garret mumbled. "I hate shitkickers and I hate shitkicking towns. The only thing in this world I hate more is friggin' Texas."

"That woman would have shot you in Maryland," Diego fumed.

"I didn't get shot in Maryland, I got shot in my damned belly. And it happened in friggin' Texas."

Someday, Neto thought, *I'm going to kill that gutless bastard.*

Neto Diego said, "Please drive us to Marshal Bowdrie's." He could not quit smiling over his excellent choice of words.

"Two men are in town looking for Pat Gunn," Spinner Olsson said, as he plopped down on his usual stool at the Happy Eagle. "Claim to be cops, but they're hired killers."

"How could you tell?" Pearl Dunbar popped the lid on a frosty bottle of Carling Black Label and prepared to measure out a third into a glass.

"I'll buy the whole bottle." Spinner laid a five-dollar bill on the bar. "Professional killers pay for information, cops beat it out of you."

"You didn't tell them anything?" Pearl's voice was tinged with trepidation.

"What's to tell? Pat went fishing."

"He'll be back."

"Reckon so." Spinner took a sip of beer. "He left the lights on at his theater and his fancy Studebaker's still there."

A cold shiver coursed through Pearl Dunbar's frame. An old wives' tale said this meant someone had walked across her future grave. The way things were going, this was frightening. First the town died, then her piano player had hung himself in a back room. Having hired killers asking about sweet Pat Gunn was simply one too many problems to allow to happen.

"Why would anyone want Pat done away with?" Pearl asked. "It's got to have to do with that arson investigator getting shot."

"Could be," Spinner said. "Or it could be they simply want to pay him money for information."

"I'm not going to take that chance!" Pearl exclaimed. She went to the phone and grabbed up the receiver. A few seconds later she yelled, "Get the hell off this line, Percy Pants. I need to make a damned important call. And if I hear you pick up to listen in, I'm heading for Wildcat Canyon with a straight razor."

"Bugger 'em!" Nero screeched. "Bugger 'em good."

"My sentiments exactly, you feathered hemorrhoid," Spinner said, proudly holding up a full bottle of beer to the parrot. No matter how hard Spinner listened, he could not make out the madam's muffled conversation. It didn't matter. He had money and, so far today, no one had turned up dead. Likely Pearl was simply ordering in more beer. At least he hoped so. The supply he had seen in the cooler appeared perilously low.

Doctor Bryce Whitlock carefully moved the thumbscrew on his comparison microscope, bringing two thirty-thirty slugs into focus. This wonderful invention, by a man named Philip Gravelle, saved a lot of eyestrain. A single microscope meant having to sketch out each land and groove, then compare them as best he could. The booming copper mining industry in Grant County had given a tax base that, thankfully, supported the purchase of modern equipment.

As are snowflakes and fingerprints, every bullet fired through a rifled barrel emerges with its own distinctive set of identifying marks. If the slug from the pig matched the bullet Sheriff Sinrod had plucked from the backseat of the car, it would clear Woody Johnson's rifle of being the murder weapon. He knew this was all a waste of time, but in government, paperwork carried a lot more weight than common sense.

"Not even close," Whitlock mumbled as he moved the two bullets around. "Now, I can have the sheriff's department return that rifle to its owner."

The coroner wondered briefly what game was in season, before deciding that was a very stupid question. Anything edible that walked about on four legs was always in season around a place like Wisdom.

Doctor Whitlock engraved each slug with his unique coroner's mark of a "W" with a line drawn horizontally across. He placed them in envelopes, which he then tossed aside to concentrate on searching for a murderer.

The Winchester rifle that he had found in the mine above Wisdom still held the empty brass cartridge that had most likely sent the lead slug flying on its mission to kill Officer Keller. He jacked the lever and removed the spent cartridge, along with five more unfired shells.

Using a pair of stainless steel forceps, the coroner lined up all six of the dull brass thirty-thirty cartridges on an examination table. Whitlock gave a silent prayer of hope, reached for his vial of fingerprint powder and began to carefully dust the shells, one at a time.

"Gotcha," he said aloud when each cartridge showed the telltale loops and swirls of very legible prints.

The next task was to transfer a copy of a full print to paper. Then would come the eye-straining chore of comparing that print to those in Sheriff Sinrod's files. He knew the chances of a match were slim, but he was a scientist. A patient man.

The coroner stood and stretched. He had been in the morgue working for too long. A bit of an outing would do him good and allow him to tie up a loose end at the same time.

Whitlock grabbed up the rifle and poked a fresh thirty-thirty shell into the loading slot.

"And another little piggy goes to market," the coroner said cheerfully, as he left the room carrying the Winchester he had found in the mine.

"Howdy gents," a rail-thin old man with white hair said after slowly extracting himself from underneath the raised hood of a gaudy Moon automobile. "If you need gas, I'll need to have Missus Bowdrie turn on the pumps."

"Are you Ronald Bowdrie?" Garret Black asked, attempting to be pleasant. His voice still came across like a growl.

"No sir," the old man said. "I'm Oliver Jordan, a friend of the Bowdries. Ronnie got an eye blown out the other day. He's on a lot of pain medicine and sleeps most of the time. He has to go to the doc, so I offered to get their car running for them."

"Nice looking cars, those Moons were," Neto Diego said from the passenger seat. "Too bad they don't make them any more."

"Parts are the problem," Jordan said. "All this one needed was a new carburetor; finding it was a real problem. I finally found one in a junkyard in Lordsburg, of all places. I put new gaskets in it, adjusted the float and now this car purrs like a contented kitten. You want me to start it so you can hear how good it runs?"

"We're state police," Neto said politely. "Here investigating the murder of Officer Keller and the assault upon the marshal. It would be quite helpful if we could speak with Mister Bowdrie."

"I'm Minnie, Marshal Bowdrie's wife, maybe I can help you," a trim, pretty woman with short brown hair said, stepping from the front door of the gas station. "Ron's asleep right now. When he's awake he's in a lot of pain and not up to answering questions."

"I understand what it feels like to be shot," Black said quickly. "We'll give him his rest."

Neto Diego added, "We would like to ask if either of you know when the theater owner, Pat Gunn, will be back from his fishing trip. There's some questions we need to ask him."

Oliver Jordan shook his white-cropped head. "That's a good one. I've lived here a long time and I didn't even know Pat Gunn owned a fishing pole. He refuses to eat fish, I know that much for certain." The old man looked at Minnie. "You ever heard of Pat doing any fishing?"

Diego and Black exchanged knowing glances. They did not need to wait for the woman's reply.

"That's all right, folks," Sergeant Black said. "We must have misunderstood is all." As he rolled up the window he added, "Thanks for your time."

Several minutes passed before either of the seething officers in the fast-moving Packard spoke. Both men knew that they had been duped, but by whom? In a red rage, they sped toward Silver City to ask some very pointed questions of the sheriff.

Garret Black got some small satisfaction from the fact that the lieutenant was in such a state of high dudgeon, he neglected his usual yelling for him to slow down.

CHAPTER TWENTY-ONE

"As fast as that idiot is driving," Woody Johnson fumed, "if he was to blow a tire, that fancy big Packard won't stop rolling until it smacks into a tree somewhere down in Mexico."

"As least he finally got around us," Carla said. "I'm anxious to get to Silver City myself, but want to make it there in one piece."

"Darlin'," Woody said, reaching over to brush the back of his hand softly across Carla's freckled cheek. "We're going to rustle us up a sky pilot right after we stop by the courthouse and buy ourselves a license to get married." He raised an eyebrow. "Then what we did last night and this morning won't be against the law. Come to think on the matter, how come the law gets a cut, anyway? What happened between us didn't cost the taxpayers a red cent."

"I've been trying to tell judges that for years. They seem too set in their ways to change, so I suppose we'll need to pay the fee."

Woody swallowed hard. It would likely be a long while before being reminded of his future wife's lurid past ceased to bother him. But the miner was going to make an honest woman of Carla Holland, real soon. Once they were married, if anyone so much as mentioned a bad word about whores, *any* whore, he planned to bust a beer bottle over their thick skull.

Last evening, on their way into Wisdom, the couple had stopped by the Angel's Roost Mine to give Carla a look at her future home. Within minutes of closing the door behind them and lighting a coal oil lamp, Woody realized his bed springs squeaked something fierce. But by then, he really could have cared less.

After a delightfully slow start this morning, the two-some had decided to go straight to Silver City and be married. Woody had stealthily fished his life savings of sixty dollars from the flour bin in the kitchen. He was going to surprise his new bride by renting a genuine hotel room for the night. Even the price of gas now seemed reasonable and all that rationing nonsense wouldn't start until the first of December. There was every good reason in the world for a celebration.

Before leaving for Silver City and their wedding, Carla had agreed to take a bath in a number two washtub without complaint. Woody Johnson knew then he had truly found a woman to keep. Floating on a satiny cloud of love scented with spring cherry blossoms, Woody continued driving toward Silver City, traveling a prosaic thirty miles an hour, which was the highest speed the worn-out old Model A truck was capable of, even on a level road.

The bright October sun was dying bloody above the gentle, rounded hills west of Silver City when Doctor Bryce Whitlock pushed away from his desk with a snort. He felt as if he had been staring at fingerprints for days, when in actuality, he had been at the task a mere two hours. He rubbed gritty eyes with the backs of his hands, then decided to go perk a fresh pot of coffee. The dark syrupy stuff that was left over from morning, he decided, was better suited for varnishing coffins.

The coroner lit a cigarette as he stood, shaking life back into his left leg, which had gone to sleep unbidden. As he puttered about the morgue trying to figure out where Maria, his secretary, had hidden the can of coffee, he mulled the findings of the case.

It came as no surprise that the bullet from the pig he shot earlier today was an identical match to the one that killed Frank Keller. He had the murder weapon.

One surprise, however, would be coming Sheriff Sinrod's way very shortly. It would be a bill for a two-hundred-eighty-pound Hampshire pig. Otto Ludwig, owner of the slaughterhouse, had insisted that, due to the coroner's killing spree, he had more pork than he could sell. The insolent German had made him agree to have the county pay for the pig before he would allow him to shoot it.

An evil grin had crossed the doctor's face when he had signed the county voucher, paying extra to have the entire pig ground into Bratwurst sausage links—with lots of extra garlic—and delivered to the sheriff's department as soon as possible.

Thinking back on the matter, the doctor realized he could have shot one pig twice and likely come up with the same results. It had simply not occurred to him to economize. Shooting two pigs, however, had given him the opportunity for a couple of delightful outings from his dreary office in the morgue to visit the slaughterhouse. Also, this course of action would be quite entertaining; Sam Sinrod hated garlic worse than a vampire.

After poking in most every shelf and cabinet in his office and coming up blank, the coroner decided to forgo making any fresh coffee. He made a mental note to find out tomorrow where Maria kept the supply of Folgers hidden, lit a Chesterfield and returned to squinting at fingerprints.

The very next set of prints from the sheriff's files that he compared to those taken from the shells in the murder weapon were a perfect match.

Whitlock bolted upright. He stared incredulously at the prints, rubbing his chin between his thumb and forefinger. This simply could not be. The doctor crushed out his smoke, deciding to make certain he had not made some error due to eyestrain or fatigue.

Upon close examination, the exact match of fingerprints was undeniable.

"Sherlock Holmes," Bryce Whitlock said, shaking his head, "this twist would keep you awake all night trying to solve. I suspect you might even need some of your seven-percent solution to help figure this one out."

The coroner hurriedly tossed what he needed into a folder and bolted for the door. He needed to get to the sheriff as quickly as possible. This turn of events was far too perplexing and confusing to delay sharing.

Pearl Dunbar sat apprehensively on a stool behind the bar at the Happy Eagle. For hours now she had been attempting to read a magazine while waiting for the telephone to ring. The longer it took to get in touch with her father in Santa Fe, the graver the danger to her love, Pat Gunn.

Her sole customer kept guzzling beer and generally rasping nerves by wheezing worse than a steam locomotive and banging that blasted silver dollar of his on the bar to watch it twirl around, only to eventually fall over with a sharp ringing sound. The distractions finally caused Pearl to toss her magazine aside. There was no way to concentrate on reading with her emotions in a jumble.

Pearl stood, lit a cigarette, then with determination set in her mind, she strode to the beer cooler, where she extracted the remaining five bottles of Carling Black Label beer. She took a moment to unplug the Frigidaire from the wall before setting the sweaty brown bottles in front of a startled Spinner Olsson.

"I really was doing just fine with one bottle at a time," said Spinner. "Those others I was planning on for later."

"The Happy Eagle's closed," Pearl said with a tinge of sadness. The old man wasn't the cause of any of her problems. "Those are the last bottles of beer I have. They're on the house."

"I didn't know you were gonna close," Spinner said with sadness in his voice. "The town's gonna miss this place."

"There's no way I can keep going. Not only did my last girl run off with your friend, Woody, there's not enough people around Wisdom anymore to keep one bar open, let alone two."

"What're you planning to do, stay here in town, or leave?"

Pearl Dunbar straightened as if she had been struck. She had no way of answering that question until she was able to talk to Pat Gunn. Her heart belonged to that sweet man who she believed was in terrible danger. If only he would have her, she knew she would be happy for the rest of her days.

While Pearl was her true first name, Dunbar was not. And she had not always been a madam, nor ever a working girl. Born into a family of means, she had received an excellent college education. After graduation with a degree in English from a prestigious eastern university, Pearl had taught literature to freshmen at the University of Colorado. Then a torrid affair with the dean had left her pregnant and the family name of Castle thoroughly scandalized.

Her sweet child had been a beautiful, loving redheaded girl. At only three months of age, her baby, Henrietta, had sadly died of pneumonia.

Alone and cut off from family, Pearl had taken her considerable savings and bought a thriving brothel in Memphis, Tennessee, where she learned to sell men what they wanted most, but make them pay through the nose to get it. This was the most satisfying form of revenge she could come up with to even things with her father.

Only the prettiest, youngest and most seductive girls worked for Pearl Dunbar. Pearl would tease the customers with alluring dresses and sexy demeanor, but never, ever, went to a room with one of them. Giving the men what they came for, she left to her working girls.

A change of mayors, from an understanding fellow who appreciated extra money and an occasional good time to a fundamentalist Baptist, had brought disaster. Within weeks of the pulpit-pounder's inauguration, Pearl's joint was raided and padlocked by sad-faced policemen who were terribly distraught over losing an excellent source of bribe money.

Pearl had begun to yearn for the serene majesty of her native New Mexico. The humidity, mosquitoes and chiggers alone were enough encouragement to leave Memphis, beside the additional pain of having to endure a narrow-minded Baptist mayor.

The Happy Eagle had done well these past few years. Very well indeed. Investments made early in Memphis and later in Wisdom, into stocks beaten down by the Depression, had grown handsomely. Pearl Dunbar, at a still-young forty-one years of age, did not need to concern herself with money matters. Closing the Happy Eagle was of no significance. She could toss some clothes into the trunk of her immaculate 1937 Cord that had been cloistered away in an adjoining garage since coming to Wisdom, and simply drive off with no regrets.

No regrets, that is, except for Pat Gunn. Of all the men she had known, he was the sweetest, the kindest of them all. His beaming smile, more the smirk of a little boy who had been up to something naughty, she found endearing. Most every man wanted only to rush a girl to bed, get what he wanted, then go about his business.

Pat Gunn had spent many, many hours talking with her. They discussed movies, books, the war, anything and everything but sex. He never had said one derogatory thing about any of her girls or the type of business Pearl was in. Neither had Pat ever gone to a room with any of the working girls. And many of them were far prettier and more tempting than Pearl Dunbar. They were also quite available. Yet Pat had eyes only for "my sweet redhead" or "sugar dumpling," as he lovingly called her.

With a state policeman being killed, Pearl did not dismiss Spinner Olsson's opinion that hired killers were asking questions to discern her lover's whereabouts.

Politics stunk worse than a sackful of dead buzzards, but a few strings pulled in the right places accomplished more than most people believed possible.

Pearl Dunbar had not pushed her family for favors before. She had always been an appalling embarrassment to their sensibilities. Since becoming a madam, she was even more certain her loving father, who had not answered any of her letters for over ten years, would not want her to go to the newspapers and divulge her real name. No, he would go to most any lengths to keep Pearl Castle from ever surfacing.

It was time to push her father into doing something to help her for once in his life. Something like keeping Pat Gunn alive. The white-haired, golden-throated bastard of a politician would do what she asked of him. He really had no choice in this matter, she mused. None at all.

Pearl sat back down on the stool and lit another cigarette. She silently watched the phone, hoping fervently it would ring soon.

Spinner Olsson grinned at his treasure trove of beer and decided Christmas had come early.

"Bugger 'em, bugger 'em," Nero kept screeching incessantly. "Get a poke, jigger the johnson."

Spinner thought if the parrot were to fall off his perch dead from a stroke, the day wouldn't turn out all that bad, even if the only whorehouse in Wisdom was closing.

The coroner nearly collided with Garret Black and Neto Diego as he rushed through the door into the sheriff's office.

"Watch it fellow!" Sergeant Black growled.

"Sorry," Doctor Whitlock said quite sincerely, after spying a large knife that had appeared in the sergeant's hand as if by magic. "I really must be more careful in the future."

"Yeah," Garret said, returning the stiletto to a hidden recess in the thick leather belt he always wore. "You do that."

"Come along, Sergeant," Neto said as if talking to a mulish dog, "we have things to do."

Garret Black once again fixed the doctor in his gaze with unblinking dark eyes that evoked images of something horrible and malevolent staring from the maw of a dank cave. "See you around," he said coldly. Then he spun and obediently followed the lieutenant down the hallway.

Whitlock shut the door behind him and turned to Sheriff Sinrod. "Those two really have a way of growing on you."

"So do warts," Sam Sinrod grumbled, thumbing through

a stack of papers on his desk. After a moment he gave up rummaging for whatever it was he was looking for, leaned back in his chair and said, "Doc, we've got problems. The state boys found out Pat Gunn's not on a fishing trip. Hell, Gunn doesn't even own a fishing pole. You should have at least asked him about that sort of thing before concocting the story."

Doctor Whitlock shrugged his shoulders. "You'll have to admit they don't *look* that smart. What did you tell them?"

"I acted shocked, of course. A small-town sheriff can't be expected to be too bright. To keep the peace I told them I would send out an arrest warrant for Pat Gunn. I also promised to call those two stooges the very moment I get a lead on where the man might be." Sinrod lowered his eyebrows. "You haven't seen Gunn lately, have you?"

"Not since breakfast. I honestly believe he's out fishing on the Gila."

"That's what I think, myself."

"They're here to kill him. There's no doubt about it."

"*Why* is the question. Al Capone and our esteemed attorney general are almost certainly involved, but I'm beginning to wonder more and more about that arson investigator. How does his being shot enter into this puzzle, which has, by the way, gotten even more bizarre?"

The sheriff leaned on the desk and cradled his hands on each side of his face. After a long moment he said forlornly, "Don't tell me that Winchester you found in the mine wasn't the murder weapon."

"Okay." The doctor grinned and lit a cigarette. "Then I won't. That was the gun, all right. The ballistics on another one of Ludwig's pigs proved it."

"You're being awfully rough on livestock lately. I hope it'll pay off."

It will if you liked garlic bratwurst, the coroner thought.

Doctor Whitlock's expression turned grim. He blew a smoke ring and watched until it disappeared at the ceiling. "I got excellent prints from every shell in the thirty-thirty that killed Officer Keller."

"But you didn't get a match from any in my files." Sinrod sighed. "That was too long of a shot to hope for, Doc."

"Sam," the coroner said severely, "that's the rub, I did get a perfect match. Those prints shouldn't be there. This beats any scenario I can come up with."

"Well, come on, spill it." The sheriff stiffened. "Whose damn prints are you talking about?"

"Marshal Ronald Bowdrie's, Sam. He'd applied for a job here six times. I compared all six applications against the prints from those shells. His prints are the only ones on the gun that shot Officer Keller."

"Hell!" Sam Sinrod's exclamation came with a gasping sigh as if someone had hit him in the stomach. "The man was driving the damn car and nearly got killed himself. He did lose an eye. Yet his gun did the killing."

Sheriff Sinrod opened a desk drawer, took out a cigar and fired it. After long moments of stone silence he looked up at the coroner and grinned. "Well, shit."

"That's what Watson thinks, too, Sherlock," said the doctor.

CHAPTER TWENTY-TWO

"Well, my dear Doctor Whitlock, I would say this entire affair has turned into a fine kettle of fish. Rotten fish at that." Sheriff Sinrod stuck out his hand from the rear booth to signal for another round of drinks.

The duo had retired to Archie's Tropicana Cocktail Lounge to speculate the latest turn of events. The atmosphere and amenities here were more inspiring and conductive to creative thought than were either the morgue or jail. Usually, the bar in the Copper Mountain Hotel was where they went to enjoy the occasional libation. With Garret Black and Lieutenant Diego rooming there, however, Archie's seemed a much more desirable choice of watering hole.

Bryce Whitlock gave a swirl to the ice in his glass of scotch. "Pat Gunn claims hailstones make scotch whiskey taste better. Personally, I can't see any need for improvement. I'm certain God drinks His Cutty Sark on regular ice."

"I'll stick with beer, it's cheaper." The sheriff nervously twirled the empty brown bottle on the table. "You've spent quite a bit of time with Gunn. What do you make of him?"

"Actually—" Whitlock finished the final sip of amber liquid, then set the glass aside. "I like the fellow. He thinks the town of Wisdom will boom again in a matter of months, but no one ever claimed optimists were sane. We've talked quite a bit about his past, especially when Pat was hijacking booze shipments from Al Capone. He honestly believes that is the only thing he's ever done that was bad enough to cause professional killers to come after him. And I think he's telling the truth."

"What about Gunn burning down his house for insurance money? I don't think something like that would look good on an application for sainthood."

The coroner grinned. "Since the mines closed in July, there have been eleven buildings burned to the ground in Wisdom. Pat setting fire to his house, if he actually did, wouldn't make him a murderer, only desperate enough to hang on by any reasonable means. I've asked him about that fire. He just grins and talks about how bad the wiring was. By all accounts, he was on Angel's Roost Mountain when his house burned. In my opinion, he set the fire smart enough to not get caught. Pat Gunn's not going to make sainthood anytime soon, but he's not the type to murder anyone. I'm sure of that."

"Abraham Lincoln thought John Wilkes Booth was a good actor and a nice guy, too." Sheriff Sinrod leaned back to allow Penelope room to set her drink tray. The voluptuous auburn-haired waitress was stunningly pretty. He paid for the drinks and gave the smiling waitress with green bedroom eyes a half-dollar tip. He made a silent vow to drop by Archie's more often. When she had glided off, Sinrod swallowed hard and said, "If I recall correctly, we came here to try to figure out how Ronald Bowdrie shot the top of Officer Keller's head off from over a thousand feet away, then ran back to his cruiser, which he was driving at the time, and poked out one of his own eyes to make himself appear innocent."

"Huh?" Both of Doctor Whitlock's eyes were glued to the departing sultry cocktail waitress. "You know, we really need to get out more often."

"I was talking about Bowdrie's prints being on those shells."

"Yeah, that was strange." The coroner craned to catch one final glimpse of Penelope. "I noticed that poor girl had a slight tremor to her hands. I should ask her to drop by my office for a physical. No charge, of course."

"Make sure to show her the eyeball and finger you keep in a jar on your desk. Dames go for guys with hobbies."

Doctor Whitlock lit a Chesterfield. Ignoring the sheriff's comment he said, "I don't think the two stooges from Santa Fe need to have that tidbit of information about the prints. They would simply claim Pat Gunn stole the rifle to throw the law off."

"That *is* a possibility, you must admit."

"Thereby hangs a tale, my dear Sherlock. Possibilities abound in *any* murder case. There are simply many different reasons Officer Keller could have been shot. But having hired killers lurking about to kill the only suspect is mind-boggling."

"You mean we're stumped."

"Using short shrift, yes."

The sheriff clucked his tongue. "My guess is Al Capone's behind this whole mess. He's paying Diego and Black to hit Gunn to get even for old grievances."

Doctor Whitlock sipped his scotch. "So two professional killers, who are likely so good at their job that the Grim Reaper sends them Christmas cards, shot a state arson investigator for practice, using a rifle they stole from Ronald Bowdrie. Then they scared the man they were paid to hit so bad he didn't argue about hiding. Not to mention the fact they have called attention of the law and news media to the case so no one would miss their killing Pat Gunn."

"Well *I* think," Sam Sinrod guzzled his bottle of beer,

"W. C. Fields was correct when he said, 'a man has to believe in something. I believe we ought to have another drink.' "

Doctor Whitlock beamed when he thought of the stunning Penelope. "I concur with your diagnosis," he said happily, craning to get the young lady's attention.

Deep shadows were filling the yawning canyons that cradled the withering town of Wisdom. Along the main street that had so recently reverberated with the sounds of music and laughter, only the plaintive cry of an evening grosbeak broke the heavy silence.

The marquee of the Starlight Theater was, for another night, becoming a beacon against the dark. A beacon very few would ever see.

Inside of the Happy Eagle Bar, Pearl Dunbar sat alone by the telephone, drinking gin and chain-smoking Pall Mall cigarettes. Old Spinner Olsson had finished his beers and shuffled off, most likely to stop by the Bloated Goat and inform the Chapmans of her closing the bar. Pearl simply didn't care.

The sharp jangling of the phone nearly caused her to spill her drink.

Pearl grabbed the receiver. From the lack of static on the line, she knew Big Jimmy Lyons was not eavesdropping on the conversation.

"Daddy," she said, "I don't need money, but I do need your help. Sit down if you're not already, because I'm going to tell you exactly what has to be done. If you don't agree, I'll be in the office of the *Santa Fe Times* in the morning with a copy of my birth certificate. I think you know I'm not one to bluff."

Pearl Dunbar talked and listened intensely. After a few

moments her expression brightened. "You will do this tonight?" she asked. Minutes later, "Thank you, *Daddy*. You're safe from having the good people of the state of New Mexico finding out that your only daughter is the madam of a whorehouse. Remember, if you had only loved and stuck by me when I became pregnant in Colorado, I wouldn't be a thorn in your side these days."

A tear trickled down her cheek, glistening like a red icicle in the lights of the bar. "No, I don't plan to ever call you again."

The clang of the black receiver striking its cradle fused with Pearl's cries of bewailment. She had not really expected so much as a single word of kindness, but she desperately had hoped for some sign, no matter how remote, that her father might actually care for her.

Truth, as Pearl Castle realized through the searing agony in her heart, can be the biggest hurt of all.

CHAPTER TWENTY-THREE

Mrs. Carla Johnson had proudly signed her new name for the second time today on the register of the Copper Mountain Hotel. The first had been on a marriage license in the courthouse where Woody Johnson and she had obtained the legal form.

Later, in a small white Presbyterian Church, there had been no flowers, no music, just a few words mouthed listlessly by a skinny old preacher in a worn suit. The ceremony had taken only minutes.

To Carla, becoming married had been the vivification of her soul. She could not look about the simple rented room without straining through happy tears. In her long years of being a working girl, Carla Holland had been inside many hotel rooms, far too many. Mostly she remembered the ceilings.

No longer would Carla have to submit to indignities suffered by a girl branded a harlot or a whore. She was now a married woman. It amazed her how quickly and easily she had given her life to a man more than twenty years her senior, a man with no money. A man whom she had not known for what most would term a respectable amount of time.

Carla Johnson did not care what others thought. For the first time in memory, she was letting her heart do the thinking. And loved the feeling.

Woody came close behind her. He brushed her hair aside and planted a tantalizing kiss on the nape of her neck. She quivered from his sweet, gentle touch.

Carla turned; her eyes widened when she saw clutched between her lover's fingers a single long-stemmed red rose. She could not comprehend how he had managed to buy the rose without her knowing.

Woody spoke so softly she had to strain to hear. "The rose is the most beautiful flower in the world. I'll give you one of these on this day, every year we're married. I want to keep your love fresh in my mind for eternity."

Carla could not answer. For a very long while all she was able to do was embrace Woody. And cry more happy tears.

Spinner Olsson coughed until he could only make gurgling noises, like water trying to drain from a nearly plugged sink.

Fred Chapman set a full glass of golden draft beer in front of the old man. "Here, clear the frog out of your throat. I could've sworn you said Pearl's closing her cathouse."

"Ain't no frog." Spinner gasped after a healthy swallow. "I got so damn much gold dust in my lungs, it'd pay the undertaker to ship my carcass to a smelter."

"From the looks of things, you're gonna outlive Wisdom," Fred said.

Spinner finished his beer and looked about; Irene was sleeping again on the bar in front of a dozen or so empty glasses. There were no other people in the Bloated Goat. The cold snap had killed off the crickets. Only the lonesome moan of an occasional gust of wind hooting in the eves of the saloon broke the unrelenting silence that now claimed the town of Wisdom.

"Where's Lonnie Dillman and all the metal scrappers?" Spinner asked. "I thought they'd be tossing money around like drunken sailors."

"No, they're going to be driving up from Silver City in the mornings, get a load of scrap and head back to unload it by nightfall. Those fellows won't be spending much money here in the Goat."

"Darn sorry to hear that, Fred. At least your hearing still works. I sure as hell said Pearl's done gone and closed the Happy Eagle. I drank the last beer she'll ever serve up there just a bit ago."

Fred Chapman staggered to the cooler, took out a fresh bottle of Carling Black Label and popped the lid. "I *really* hate to hear that. The Godfreys pulled out today, too. They stopped by to tell us they were leaving and let us know there's some flour, sacks of pinto beans and such they left up at their restaurant. Anyone can help themselves; they didn't even bother to lock the door. Now you go and tell me the cathouse has closed. I reckon there's only us and Pat Gunn left to hang on trying to run a business here in Wisdom."

"You old poop." Irene had roused to an upright position. "We ain't leaving here or giving up. This town'll boom again right soon. You'll see."

"Yes, dear." Fred's voice was dull, lifeless. "I'm sure you're right."

The cold wind buffeting through Angel's Roost Canyon hooted in the eves of the bar until Fred could not stand the mournful noise any longer. He clicked on the radio. Once it had warmed up, he turned the dial on the eleven-tube Crosley to the clearest station they could receive in this steep canyon. News of the war in Europe was on. People dying by the thousands in German bombing raids told him that he was not alone in his despair.

"The Japs are who shot Officer Keller." Sheriff Sinrod's words were somewhat slurred, which complemented his glazed eyes. "I'm betting that's the straight scoop. Those sneaky yellow sons of guns went and sent in a sniper just to whack that arson investigator for no other reason than to confuse the hell outta us."

"Huh?" Doctor Whitlock was craning to get yet another peek at the beautiful Penelope Leathers. Already there was a sharp crick in his neck, but the lovely lass was deserving of every lustful, painful moment he could muster. With each drink, the coroner had become more and more infatuated with the sexy, green-eyed waitress.

"Oh nothing," Sam said. "I only mentioned that your car was on fire."

Bryce Whitlock quickly turned his gaze to the sheriff. Instantly he wished he had moved slower, much slower. His neck burned as if it was on fire. "My mind was wandering, wasn't it?"

"That's okay," Sam said. "Even when it's about, it's doing its thinking below the beltline." He grinned. "The signs are obvious, Watson, you have been smitten with lust. I shall remove myself to my home and allow your pursuit of basic urges to proceed unimpeded. Besides, a sheriff should never be seen drinking more than a dozen beers in public. That might possibly do damage to my image."

"I suggest we meet in the morning for breakfast at Ellie's Diner." The doctor appeared irritatingly sober, as he always did whenever they went out drinking. "You should also phone the Army and report that Jap sniper. I'm sure you'll be downright surprised at all of the attention you'll get."

The sheriff came to his feet and looked around to get his bearings. Attempting to leave a cocktail lounge by way of a broom closet could cost him votes come the next election. "Penelope Leathers, my good man, I leave in your capable hands. Don't do anything I wouldn't do."

"No chance of that." Whitlock leered. "Whatever that might be isn't in a French dictionary. Thinking on the matter, I doubt if a person could find it in a Turkish dictionary, either."

"You're just getting uppity because I'm better looking than you."

Whitlock grinned evilly. "If I'm late for breakfast, go ahead and start without me. I recommend anything with pork."

A heavy hand made its presence known on Sheriff Sinrod's shoulder. He turned to blink his eyes into focus on Burke Martin, one of his deputies.

"Sorry to bother you, boss," Burke said, glancing furtively at the profusion of empty brown beer bottles littering the table. "But something's come up I thought you should know about. I saw your car outside and well—"

"Come out with it, man," Sinrod said. "The coroner and I've been here discussing business is all."

Doctor Whitlock coughed into his handkerchief to mask a snicker.

Deputy Marin said, "It's about that Pat Gunn fellow, sir. You'd asked us to quietly keep an eye on him while he's staying at the Doc's place."

All traces of humor fled the coroner's face.

Sheriff Sinrod's expression tightened. Suddenly sober, he regretted not letting his friend know that he had ordered surveillance on his house while Gunn was there. "Yes, go ahead."

"Well sir," the deputy strained for words. "He's gone. Pat Gunn's shagged ass for town. I was looking for him when I saw your car parked in front of this joint."

Doctor Whitlock asked, "How do you know he's come to town?"

"Oh, he left a note taped to the door. Gunn said he was walking downtown to get something good to eat and have a drink or two."

The sheriff's eyebrows drew together in a frown as he focused on the coroner. "You made that poor man eat *your* cooking. I should've shown Pat Gunn some compassion and thrown him in jail, which was my first plan, come to think back on the situation."

Doctor Whitlock stuck out a hand, palm open. "Where's the best place in town to get a really good meal?"

"Everyone knows that would be." Sam's eyes widened when realization of the facts crashed past the alcohol. "The Copper Mountain Hotel; my God that's where Garret Black and Neto Diego are staying!"

Doctor Whitlock bolted to his feet. He took a moment to fish a dollar bill from his wallet and tuck it under an empty glass as a tip for sweet Penelope before joining in the rush to the hotel.

CHAPTER TWENTY-FOUR

Pat Gunn was stunned to see Woody Johnson's battered old Model A Ford truck in the parking lot of the Copper Mountain Hotel. The old miner was so tight with money he would squeeze a penny hard enough to make Abraham Lincoln sing soprano. And the Copper Mountain was noted for being an expensive place to stay or eat a meal.

After a moment of staring at Woody's truck, Pat clucked his tongue and continued on his way to the lounge. If Woody was in the hotel, that was most likely where he could be found.

Pat had decided during the strenuous, mile long walk from Doctor Whitlock's house that a single drink—or maybe three at the most—would hold him until he had a decent dinner tucked behind his belt buckle. The coroner was a decent enough fellow, but without a doubt the worst cook in New Mexico, with Colorado and Arizona tossed in for good measure.

That afternoon Pat had pondered warming up, for the third time, a pan of boiled cabbage with rutabagas and celery along with some fried pork livers against a sumptuous steak dinner at a good restaurant. The dullest village idiot in history would have made the same decision he had. The very idea that he was in danger from Al Capone was a silly notion. On the other hand, both the coroner and sheriff seemed concerned. This was bothersome, unless they had blown up the affair to keep him out of their way for awhile, but why?

After sniffing the gray liver, Pat had thrown caution to the wind. The chances were no one in Silver City would know who he was anyway. He had eaten a few times in the hotel and enjoyed it very much. A huge, juicy medium-rare Porterhouse steak with all of the trimmings, along with a huge slice of cherry pie à la mode for dessert and a few drinks in the bar would certainly cost as much as two dollars. Possibly more. Money, however, is of absolutely no use to a man who had died from eating rutabagas and rancid hog liver.

The cocktail lounge in the Copper Mountain was bustling with business, as usual. Pat stood for a moment scouring the crowd for any sight of Woody Johnson. Briefly, he felt a pang of regret, remembering that not so long ago, Wisdom had been this vibrant, this *alive*. He brightened when he reminded himself the lull of business in his hometown was only temporary.

Woody Johnson did not appear to be in the lounge and Pat was too hungry to concern himself with finding him until after his repast. He made his way to the bar, walking past a table where he observed a man wearing a state policeman's uniform crack a raw egg into a glass and then begin gleefully sipping at it.

Pat shuddered at the thought of eating a raw egg. Perhaps, he mused, the town of Silver City was becoming infested with people who had lost their bearings when it came to eating wholesome, good-tasting food.

"What'll be your pleasure, Mister Gunn?" the ponderous bartender sporting an old-fashioned handlebar moustache asked cheerfully and loudly. "I'm afraid we're completely out of hailstones."

Pat cocked his head in surprise and regarded the chubby waiter. "Well if it isn't Ben Appel. I haven't seen you for a coon's age. When you closed your hardware store in Wisdom, I'd have thought you'd gone farther than here."

"Can't imagine why I'd want to do that," Ben said. "I like the country; besides, tending bar pays better than working for myself. The hours are better, too. What I'd like to know is, when's Pat Gunn going to get smart enough to head for greener pastures? Wisdom ain't nothing but a ghost town these days."

"Scotch whiskey, the best cheap stuff you've got. A double shot over regular ice." Pat's expression was one of a traffic cop listening to someone try and talk their way out of a speeding ticket. "Ben, this war will be over real soon. Then you can quit having fun and move back to Wisdom. Go back and work at an honest trade, like selling hardware for six prices."

Ben Appel poured the drink with a flourish, set it in front of Pat on a white napkin, then headed down the busy bar to take care of other customers.

Pat sipped at the scotch and sincerely wished hailstones were available. He pitied men like Ben. Men who had given up so easily on the wonderful town of Wisdom. Anyplace has its ups and downs. The secret of success is to stay the course. Any idiot knows that to be true.

"Excuse me sir," the large, neatly dressed Mexican man who had been sitting with the raw egg-eating cop stood behind him. "I could not help but overhear. Are you the Mister Pat Gunn, who owns the Starlight motion picture theater in Wisdom?"

Pat gave a blank, stunned look. He hadn't expected to be recognized by anyone in Silver City. The way the evening was going, he should run for mayor.

"Who's asking?" Pat said cautiously.

"State police business, sir." The Mexican produced a

shiny silver badge declaring him to be Lieutenant Neto Diego.

"Yeah, I'm Pat Gunn," Pat said with a dismissive shrug. If a person can't trust the police, who can he trust?

"We have been looking for you, sir." Diego motioned to the skinny, dour man sipping a glass of raw eggs. "Sergeant Black and I are most concerned for your safety. We need to get you to a safer place right away."

Pat sighed and chugged his scotch. "I've been hearing that a lot lately. But I'm not going anywhere with anybody until I get a doggone steak dinner."

Lieutenant Diego looked about furtively. "Yes, Mister Gunn, if you insist. But Garret Black and I must accompany you, then I insist that we see to your safety at some other, more secure, place than here."

Pat said, "Do you intend to feed me liver and rutabagas?"

"No." Neto's dusky face expressed puzzlement. "Not at all, sir."

"Then once I have my steak," Pat said, "I'm all yours."

Ben Appel draped a clean towel over his arm, adjusted his bow tie in the huge mirror that lined the back bar then went to see what Sheriff Sinrod wanted. The bartender had never seen the sheriff's face quite so tense and ruddy. It was obvious something big was going down to cause the coroner, along with Deputy Martin, to accompany Sinrod. All of the men wore tight expressions of anxiety. Briefly, Ben wondered if they were here to ask embarrassing questions about the profitable, late night, high stakes poker games held in the Elks lodge that he presided over. He relaxed when he remembered the lodge had contributed very generously to Sheriff Sinrod's election campaign.

"Evening Sheriff," Ben said cheerfully. "Would you gents care for a drink? Remember, for all local officers of the law the first drink's always on the house."

Doctor Whitlock said, "Ben, you know Pat Gunn from up in Wisdom?"

"Sure Doc. Most everyone knows him."

"He's in dire danger," Sinrod said sharply. "We have reason to believe he might be here in the hotel."

"Sure was," Ben Appel said. "Old Woody Johnson from Wisdom's here too. Would you believe that old coot's in the honeymoon suite? Woody's gone and married up with one of Pearl Dunbar's girls half his age." He chuckled. "I reckon sap rises in an old tree same as a sprout."

"Pat Gunn!" Sinrod growled. "Where *is* he?"

The barkeep shrugged dismissively. "Heck, Pat's in good hands. There's no reason to work yourselves into a dither. He had a couple of drinks then scarfed down our biggest steak dinner like he hadn't eaten for a week. Those two state lawmen who're staying here went and bought it for him. I overheard them telling Pat he was in danger, too. Being in the hands of the law, I'm sure he'll be safe as a baby in its crib."

"I take it the name Lindbergh doesn't ring a bell," Coroner Whitlock said tensely. "*Where* is Pat Gunn?"

"You ought to learn to relax more," Ben Appel said. "Folks just don't have any patience these days." He saw the sheriff's blue eyes darken into slits and decided this was not a good time for banter. "Lieutenant Diego and Garret Black left with him about—um." Ben turned to an old regulator clock on the wall. "Maybe a half-hour ago at most. Ain't no reason for concern, Pat was laughing and joking with those two all the while."

"Just like a Judas goat in Ludwig's Slaughterhouse."

Doctor Whitlock slumped dejectedly. "My God, what have I done?"

A tangerine moon hung lazily over the black, lapping waters of Palm Island, Florida. On the terrace of his palatial estate, Al Capone relaxed at a desk set up beside the kidney-shaped pool, poring over correspondence.

Capone loved the nights. Daylight hurt his eyes more and more. The dark of night also masked the festering red sores on his forehead and nose that the stupid doctors were unable to cure.

Don't those fools know who I am, he thought bitterly. *I deserve better than this. Much better.*

From this luxurious villa, Al Capone still ran a multi-million-dollar-a-year crime syndicate. At least in his mind he did. When the fog in his fevered, syphilitic brain cleared, as on occasion it would, he remembered past wrongs. And he had money at his disposal. Lots and lots of cold hard cash that he had successfully hidden from the greedy United States Government.

How dare they call me a tax cheat and put me in prison with common criminals.

Al Capone was not a man to let bygones be bygones. Using a thin ivory letter-opener, he slit open an official-looking letter from the State of New Mexico. The enclosed letter was from Attorney General Jack Sutton, politely requesting a donation to help him run for the Senate.

The putrefying sores on his forehead glistened in the tawny moonlight as Capone grinned and wrote Sutton a five-thousand-dollar check. Discretion was the byword for a man on parole. There was nothing amiss about helping out an aspiring politician who was an old friend and his past lawyer. Should the arrogant upstart, Pat Gunn, who once stole many valuable truckloads of whiskey from him, suffer a fatal accident, well, that would just be too bad.

Using the same stationery he had for many years, he folded the check inside with a note of encouragement from Alphonse Capone, Secondhand Furniture Dealer, 2222 S. Wabash, Chicago, Illinois. Often he had to remind himself that he was no longer in Chicago. Sometimes he forgot the simplest of things.

Capone clucked his tongue when he remembered he had forgotten to pay a snitch. In his line of endeavor, information was more important that gold. He wrote out another check for one hundred dollars to Phylo Norton. The little man was worthless as a forger, but his report of Pat Gunn's whereabouts had been quite accurate. And Al Capone would never welch on a honest debt.

"Max," Capone called out.

What had appeared to be a shadow beside a palm tree turned into a hulking man carrying a submachine gun.

"Yeah boss."

"Take these two letters to the mailbox."

"Sure boss."

"Then tell Sheila and Doreen to come to me. I won't be needing you anymore tonight."

The man nodded, scooped up the envelopes and faded once again into undulating shadows. Max had often wondered what some women would do for money. Now that he knew, he felt sickened.

CHAPTER TWENTY-FIVE

For Pearl Dunbar the night passed slowly as molasses poured in January. What little sleep she received came in fleet, stolen moments. All she could do was fret and worry over the safety of her sweet Pat Gunn.

Bernard Shunny, the dean of the University of Colorado, had been the first man she had given her love to. Bernie had wined and dined, then deflowered, her. Oh, he had whispered many sweet nothings in her ear, promised her marriage and a golden future. Never once had the vile opportunist even alluded to having a wife and five children. Pearl had trusted that man with all of her heart and soul, only to be shamed. Then baby Henrietta had come along and built castles of love that, oh so soon, had crashed to dust.

Now she had allowed herself to fall hopelessly in love with Pat Gunn. Pearl silently chided herself for reaching out once again with her heart. A person who remains alone shields herself from much of the anguish to be suffered in this brutal world. But loneliness demands its own terrible price. And love is something that must be given, before it can be received.

All through the long, silent night, until the red rays of dawn peeked over the eastern horizon, Pearl tossed and turned, mulled and fretted. The light of day awoke Nero. The parrot's shrill squawking grated like fingernails scraped across a windowpane. For the first time she realized why so many customers had wished for the macaw's early demise.

Pearl shook the sleep from her eyes. She arose, bathed and dressed. Waiting was all she could do. Nero was only an irritating bird, but he depended on her. It was better than being alone.

Cold shadows were filling the canyons that cradled Wisdom when Woody and Carla's Model A squalled to a stop in front of the Bloated Goat Saloon.

Irene bolted upright from her usual nap on the bar. Business being what it was, she could think of no good reason to wait until late in the day for a drink. "What in the name of blazes was that?"

Fred Chapman came trudging from the back room where he had been taking inventory. He peered out the front window, smiled and waited until Woody was inside to say, "Those brakes squeal worse than a mountain lion being nutted with a rusty knife. I'd be investing in a heavy anchor and a short rope if you don't get 'em fixed soon."

Woody said, "I plan on getting around to that someday. Lately, I've been sorta busy." He stepped aside and scooped a beaming Carla into the crook of his arm. "Meet my new bride, Carla Johnson. We got hitched yesterday in Silver City."

Irene hopped from the barstool, beaming proudly at Woody's wife. "I swear, child, you've gone and got yourself one good man. This town'll boom again right shortly and you'll do just fine. There's a lot of rich ore in that Angel's Roost Mine of yours, too. I'm so proud of you two I'm gonna fix you both mint juleps, on the house."

A stunned Fred Chapman went and grabbed a beer from the cooler to give himself time to think of something to say. He really wanted to give Woody his sympathies, but doubted this would be a good time to do so. Fred popped the top of his bottle and remembered back on six months of blissful marriage. The problem was, that had been nearly fifty years ago.

"Congratulations, you two," Fred said after a long swallow. "I'd venture this'll come as a right decent surprise to a lot of folks."

Woody helped Carla onto a stool and took the seat alongside her. "Speaking of surprising folks, when's Pat coming home, I wonder? He's been gone on that fishing trip for quite a while."

Fred shook his head sadly. "Come on, Woody. Pat's no fisherman. He took off with that coroner fellow from Silver City. Then some more cops came here asking questions about Pat. Spinner did manage to clean 'em out of a five-spot for telling them nothing. He keeps ranting they were professional killers. That old guy gets some strange ideas in his head sometimes. I reckon until the murder of that cop gets solved, the flat-feet will keep poking around."

Woody ignored Fred to turn and lovingly stroke Carla's freckled cheek. The signs were plain that any problems Pat Gunn or anybody else had were none of his concern, nor would they be for some time.

"Mint juleps, child," Irene said, happily crushing wilted green leaves in a porcelain mortar and pestle, "will keep you from getting sick up here in the high country. I never so much as get a case of the sniffles since I started drinking them."

"No natural germs are tough enough to get past all that mean," Fred said seriously. "But she has drank up enough whiskey that I can save money on embalming fluid when she croaks."

"Oh, you old poop," Irene said, adding precious powdered sugar to the drinks. "These kids are just starting out being married. Don't go acting like it's *all* bad." She grinned mischievously. "We *still* have our good times."

A smile crossed Fred's face. He stepped close to Irene and pecked a kiss on her wrinkled cheek. "She's mean and old, but she's all I got."

"Simmer down, you old poop." There was a twinkle in Irene's eyes. "Spooning will have to wait until after we're closed."

A couple of drinks later, Fred Chapman said to Woody, "You know that Joe Godfrey and Harriet pulled out?"

Woody sighed. "Darn, I hate to hear that. They had a mighty good restaurant and Harriet baked the best apple pies a person ever smacked their lips over."

"They mentioned there's some flour and stuff left in their place," Irene said. "The restaurant's not locked. You two might want to see what all it amounts to. Joe told us they're going to let the county have the joint for taxes and they've taken everything they're going to and to help ourselves. Florida's where they're heading for."

"Spinner dropped by last night to tell us Pearl's closed the Happy Eagle." Fred finished his beer and tossed the bottle into a wastebasket full of empties with a crash. "I know she was competition for our bar, but when a town loses its last whorehouse, that's a mighty sad occasion."

Carla started to say something, only to have the words freeze on her lips when the door opened. All eyes turned to Minnie Bowdrie. The marshal's wife seldom left their house or gas station. Ron had voiced his opinion many times that a woman's place was in the home.

Carla noticed something about Minnie the others did not. The way the pretty girl's wide, blue eyes darted about, like those of a beaten pet dog or cat, spoke of being repeatedly whipped for no reason she could understand. In

Carla's past profession it was not an uncommon expression to behold on girls new to the business, before they became hardened and devoid of emotion.

Like I used to be, Carla thought.

"Why hello, Minnie," Irene said. "Come over here, child, and join us. It does my heart good to see you out and about." She hesitated. "How's Ron doing?"

Minnie came to the bar, but did not take a seat. "Mister Chapman, sir, could I please have a bottle of beer to drink? I can't bear not getting out for a little while. Ronnie must have been hurt worse than we figured. He takes the doc's medicine and sleeps all the time. There's no reason to keep the gas station open—not a single customer's stopped by for days."

Fred went to the white Frigidaire and returned with two opened, frosty bottles of Carling Black Label. He set one in front of Minnie, reserving the other for himself. "Thanks for coming by. We'd sure like to see more of you. I'd reckon it gets mighty lonesome over there for you."

Minnie said nothing. She grabbed up the bottle and began drinking.

Woody proudly wrapped his arm around Carla's shoulder. "We just got hitched yesterday in Silver City. I'm plumb sorry to hear Slow—uh, Ron's—still out of sorts. I was thinking maybe all of us still here in Wisdom oughtta get together for maybe a few drinks and a potluck supper to help celebrate the occasion."

"Why that's a great idea," Irene said. "We can hold it right here in the Goat."

Minnie Bowdrie focused on her beer as if no one had spoken. "The gas station's been sold. Didn't get much out of it at all."

"My goodness child," Irene said. "That's awful news.

The way things are going, Fred and I'll have the only business left in Wisdom. That is, if Pat Gunn shuts down the Starlight."

"Could I please have another beer?" Minnie fished a silver dollar from a patched pocket on her red flannel shirt and daintily laid it on the bar. "I'd like to buy Woody and his wife a drink, too. It—it's nice to see folks smile." Minnie stood motionless, staring at Woody for a long moment. "Mister Johnson, the law thinks Pat Gunn killed that state policeman, don't they?"

Lines of tension furrowed Woody's brow. "Why yes, I'd reckon so. But that's the way lawmen think. They'll most always go for the easy pickings to blame someone. Whenever the real killer's found, things will be fine for Pat."

Fred said, "Terrible about that poor officer being shot like he was. I hope they find out who did it real soon. I only wish they still hung murderers. Whoever shot that cop would really draw a big crowd for their hanging. If they held it here, it'd be great for business."

Minnie gave a sob, turned and ran out, leaving the door swinging in the wind.

"You old poop," Irene growled. "The little woman's husband was nearly killed himself in that shooting. You should've kept your trap shut."

"I didn't mean anything," Fred said contritely.

Woody went and closed the door against the cold breeze. "Minnie's always been afraid of her own shadow. I'd expect all that talk of shootings and hangings was a tad more than she could take. On a happier note, I see Spinner's heading this way. He's got a couple of hundred feet to go, so I reckon we can finish this round before he shows up."

Carla said, "I hope that lady's all right. She's mighty pretty, but I can tell life's been tough for her."

"She'll be just fine, darlin'," Woody said hopping back on the stool. "Selling the station and facing moving away has got her upset is all."

"Yes dear, I'm sure you're right about her being fine," Carla said. She could not keep from worrying over Minnie Bowdrie, whose darting fear-filled eyes had sent disturbing quakes through her newfound serenity. "At least I hope so."

"They've got him!" Sheriff Sam Sinrod said sharply. He was as angry with himself as anyone else for allowing something like this to happen. "Those killers who wear a badge have absconded with Pat Gunn. It's only a matter of time until we get a call that Gunn was killed trying to escape police custody."

"It's all my fault." Doctor Whitlock was genuinely upset. Both he and the sheriff had spent the entire day either on the telephone or combing the town of Silver City for Pat Gunn or Diego and Black's showy Packard Super Eight. They sat in the coroner's office comparing notes.

"The state boys checked out of the Copper Mountain last night." Sinrod lit a cigar. "We know Pat Gunn was with them and that they bought him dinner. Then nothing. No one saw them leave town, but the hotel register shows Neto and Garret checking out at ten-thirty. After that, they drop off the face of the earth."

"Along with Pat Gunn, who was *my* responsibility."

"Don't be too hard on yourself, Doc. Both of us told him to stay put."

"I should have laid in some different food for him to eat. Ellie's Diner has good take-out. Pork liver and rutabagas are an acquired taste."

"No one will ever see it on the menu of any restaurant that'll be in business for more than a day."

Doctor Whitlock opened a fresh pack of Chesterfields, tapped out a cigarette and lit it off the stub of another. "The one thing we're not concentrating on is who killed Officer Keller. Pat Gunn didn't do it. I'm certain of that. There is a possibility Neto Diego and Garret Black are actually here to investigate a murder, not kill Pat Gunn for Al Capone. That entire scenario is too bizarre to be true."

"But my dear Watson, the obvious is very often the truth."

The coroner leaned back in his swivel rocker and sighed. "And you haven't been able to get through to the attorney general?"

"His secretary, who has all the charms of a grizzly bear suffering with piles, keeps informing me that the esteemed Jack Sutton will return my call at his earliest convenience, which will likely be a day or two after hell freezes over."

"And the governor left this morning for a vacation in California. How convenient."

"There are enough loose ends in this case to send Sherlock Holmes to the loony bin." Sinrod tapped ashes from his cigar. "Officer Keller was dying from a brain tumor. I've checked, and all the life insurance he carried was the standard five thousand dollars issued to state police. For some reason I still think his death must be tied in somehow."

"Could be," Whitlock said. "What bothers me most of all is the way the bigwigs up in Santa Fe are acting. Instead of the bevy of lawmen we expected, we get an egg-sucking hit man and a chubby Mexican chow hound who seems to hold the leash."

"But now they have Pat Gunn, the only suspect. Convenient that Gunn has a checkered past, along with having the distinction of *really* pissing off Al Capone some years ago."

The coroner coughed and took another puff on his Chesterfield. "Marshal Bowdrie's fingerprints being on those shells in the murder weapon are a puzzle we've not yet investigated. Doctor Cleary said Bowdrie was due to see him yesterday, but didn't show. He tried to call then only to find the phone's been disconnected."

"I think we ought to take a drive to Wisdom tomorrow and have a chat with the marshal. It'd be a grand idea to also shake a few trees while we're there, see what or who falls out. That Woody Johnson fellow would be a good place to start."

Doctor Whitlock sighed. "We might as well go. There's nothing to be gained by waiting around here except a case of coffee nerves. I wonder as to how much we'll get out of the marshal. Cleary's got him taking enough Phenobarbital to flatten a moose."

Sheriff Sinrod pictured the ponderous Ronald Bowdrie in his mind. "That dose sounds about right."

"In the morning then. Right after breakfast at Ellie's." Doctor Whitlock's gray eyes rolled pensively. "Sam, you were right to keep surveillance on Pat Gunn. I only wish I'd done my job as good."

Sinrod thought a moment. "Doc, we both are doing the best we can. Gunn chose to leave, and we don't know what's happened to him." The sheriff stood and went to the door. He did not turn as he said over his shoulder before leaving, "We *will* solve this case, Watson."

Slightly past one o'clock in the morning, a long, ebony, 1926 Moon automobile slowly threaded its way through the inky blackness of a cloudy night as it headed west over Angel's Roost Pass, leaving Wisdom. Sometimes the driver would miss a gear, sending metallic grating noises echoing off craggy cliffs.

The Moon Diana pulled to a dusty stop at a mail drop in the tiny town of Alma. A blur as a hand deposited a single letter. Gears ground, then the big car headed north, leaving a cloud of dust in its wake. The faster the automobile got from Wisdom, the faster it traveled. Like an animal escaping from a cage, the driver needed convincing that they were truly free before allowing themselves to run.

CHAPTER TWENTY-SIX

Pat Gunn had never been in Santa Fe before. He had come into New Mexico through El Paso and stayed in the southern part of the state ever since. The capital seemingly hummed with activity. At least the small area he could see from his window on the third floor of the Adobe Walls Hotel appeared busy.

The fact that the policemen had him locked in, he found somewhat unsettling. Then again, if Al Capone really had sent out hired killers to get him, it would not be wise to go sightseeing.

On the good side, Neto and Garret had allowed him to order room service any time he wished. Santa Fe certainly had some great restaurants. The tequila drinks weren't bad either. Nor was the delightfully cold Mexican beer. Pat found he really didn't miss scotch whiskey over hailstones all that much. Variety, he reminded himself, is the spice of life.

Pat sipped a margarita while poring over the large, leather-bound menu. Glen Miller's band played "Careless" on the radio. In a walnut bookcase were several novels to read. He hadn't read Ernest Hemingway's *For Whom the Bell Tolls*. He decided to start it this evening, right after a delicious plate of trout almondine, or possibly some stacked green chili enchiladas with two eggs, over easy, on top. The way the orange egg yolks trickled through the spicy filling made enchiladas taste so delectable.

Decisions, decisions. Pat Gunn decided he could only

stand such treatment at the hands of the state police for several more days before complaining. Thinking on the matter, he could come up with no good reason to rush back to Wisdom until the war was over and he was truly safe from Al Capone.

Stacked green chili enchiladas, fried apple pie, two or three more margaritas, along a few Tecate beers for later, it would be. Pat wore a grin when he picked up the phone to call room service. The police in New Mexico were certainly much nicer than any of those ill-tempered lawmen he had dealt with in Illinois. It had to be the weather. Chicago was cold enough in the wintertime to freeze the balls off a brass monkey. New Mexico was truly an enchanting state in which to live.

Sergeant Garret Black was in a funk. He sipped at his glass of Early Times bourbon, then turned to Lieutenant Diego, who was happily eating his way through an entire mince pie.

"This settles it," Black said firmly. "I'm gonna take my retirement and move to Montana. Maybe I'll buy a little farm and raise chickens."

"Why, your grocery bill would be practically nothing," Neto said seriously over a mouthful of mincemeat.

The gibe did not seem to register with Sergeant Black, who said, "When things go haywire as this hit's gone and done, it's high time to change occupations. Used to be really simple; you get a contract, find the mark and whack 'em. Make it look like an accident and maybe get a bonus. Then someone like Pat Gunn comes along and throws everything outta kilter."

"This *is* a unique situation, I must admit. But don't despair. I think perhaps you may get to shoot Mister Gunn, yet." Neto chuckled over his brilliant choice of words. "The attorney general *did* tell us to dispose of him."

"Yeah." Garret slumped in his chair dejectedly. "Then the governor himself calls up and tells us that Pat Gunn's got people out to kill him and then orders us to keep him safe. Up until the phone rang, I thought *we* were the ones Gunn needed to be concerned about."

Neto Diego wiped crumbs from his mouth with a white napkin. "I admit this is a strange turn of events, Sergeant. Our boss, whose name you will never mention, is attempting to reach the governor and get to the bottom of this. We do know that the governor's office did, for some unknown reason, order us to protect Pat Gunn. It is just too bad we couldn't have done the hit right away. After a mark is killed, anyone changing their mind isn't an option."

Sergeant Black said, "That arson investigator, Frank Keller, getting shot when he did would make a perfect cover. Pat Gunn being a suspect, pulling a pistol on me, then getting fatally plugged by a courageous law enforcement officer forced to defend himself is too good to pass on." Garret sighed. "We'd have gotten a good bonus, too."

Lieutenant Diego stuck his fork into the remaining piece of pie, then cocked his head in thought. "You know, whoever shot Officer Keller *did* make Pat Gunn a murder suspect. I'm beginning to think Governor Castle might be on to something about a hit being ordered on our mark. Sergeant, get to his room. Drape heavy blankets over the windows. Take a chair and stay outside his door. Check and double check everyone going in. We have a reputation to uphold."

Garret Black slugged down the last of his whiskey as he came to his feet; his dark eyes flashed like lighting from an approaching storm. "I'll take care of it, sir. Having other hit men after someone we've been sent to kill plain ain't right.

I'll see to protecting Pat Gunn until it's time for *me* to whack him." He clucked his tongue. "I sure miss the good ol' days when doing away with folks wasn't so blasted complicated."

Lonnie Dillman had difficulty keeping his eyes off Carla Johnson. The metal scrapper thought she was absolutely, stunningly beautiful. Yet when Woody's new wife was working at the Happy Eagle and readily available, Lonnie had barely noticed her. Now, he sincerely regretted not spending a couple of dollars back when opportunity could have knocked. Carla's full red lips glistened in the sunlight, complementing her firm breasts and lithe figure. The blonde's blue eyes twinkled like the finest diamonds . . .

"Well sir," Woody said cheerfully, handing back a stack of weight tickets, bringing Dillman's reverie to an end. "I reckon you done all right for the both of us. The Missus and me can find plenty of good uses for three hundred and twelve bucks."

Lonnie kicked his left boot against a tree to bring his mind into focus. "Leg went to sleep. I hate it when that happens." He jerked his gaze from Carla and headed for the truck. "If we agree that figure's correct, I'll write you a check."

"Sure sounds like a right fair figure to me." Woody twisted his thumb and forefinger against his stubble-bearded chin. "Uh, Lonnie, I was wondering if you'd consider doing something for me. I'd be paying for it."

"What might that be?" Lonnie kept his attention on writing the check. "I'll do anything I can to help you folks out."

"The Missus and me ordered a bathtub from Sears and Roebuck in Silver City. When it comes in, I need to get the thing hauled out and some help getting it inside. Those blame things weigh like a Hungarian lunch."

Lonnie tore out the check. When he turned to hand it to the old miner, his eyes snagged on winsome Carla. "Uh, sure. I'll be glad to do that for you two." He swallowed hard. "And there won't be no charge."

"Why thanks," Woody turned and solemnly stared across the valley to the sprawling Hidden Treasure Mine. "I was wondering how your big job there's going. I suspect you'll be working here for quite a spell."

"Not all that long," the scrapper's voice was tinged with disappointment. "Ira Tischler phoned and was worried we weren't moving fast enough. To be agreeable, I've sublet the contract to a big outfit from Salt Lake City. They should be here by tomorrow with at least three dozen men, along with a string of heavy trucks, trailers and a crane. I reckon within a few weeks at most, all that'll be left on that mountainside will be a memory. The Willis Brothers are going to take everything, including the wood and sheet tin, too, even the rusty stuff."

"I was sorta hoping you'd be working here all winter."

"Ira Tischler's mighty concerned about the war effort. He told me that folks can rebuild everything if we win. But if we lose, it doesn't make sense to not have thrown everything we own at 'em first."

"I'd reckon Tischler makes good sense. Being smart is likely why he got to be president of a big outfit in the first place. Still, it's sad to see things that took years to build torn down in such short order."

"That's war, I reckon." Lonnie shrugged and turned to his truck. "Leave word at the Bloated Goat when your tub's in. I'll drop by there once in a while."

"You come back and see us," Woody said.

Lonnie climbed into the cab of his Reo, shifted the noisily idling truck into gear. He bathed one last moment in Carla Johnson's beauty. It amazed him how the plain-looking girl who used to sell herself for a couple of dollars had bloomed into such a lovely lady. "I'll be happy to," he said as the big tires on his truck began crunching on loose gravel, and he was gone.

"There's one nice fellow," Woody said.

"I never noticed," Carla purred. "Not when you're around."

Woody wrapped an arm around his wife's narrow waist. "Let's go to the Goat and celebrate being rich. There might be a chance Fred can cash this check, save us from setting up a dang bank account and going all the way to Silver."

Carla pecked a kiss on her husband's cheek. "I like the Chapmans. Perhaps they might have heard from your friend, Pat. I wish he would show up. The mean old sheriff and coroner questioning you and bothering poor Mister Bowdrie about that shooting like they did needs to stop."

Woody's eyebrows drew together. "You know, Pat *has* been fishing for quite a few days now. I'd venture that no matter how good those fish are biting, he ought to be home right soon. Then things will get back to normal."

"I love the way he keeps the marquee lit up all the time. It makes the entire town look alive."

Woody clucked his tongue and looked sadly across the canyon at the extensive buildings that marked the Hidden Treasure Gold Mine. "We'd best hope it takes. Now, let's go have that drink."

CHAPTER TWENTY-SEVEN

Phylo Norton was putting in a late night working in the back room of the cigar store he maintained on West Maxwell street in Chicago. The store functioned wonderfully as a front for his growing business of forging ration stamps. The little man with salt-and-pepper hair had just completed a set of plates to allow the easy and rapid manufacture of counterfeit gasoline stamps, when a pair of brutish men wearing gray trench coats came crashing through the door.

Disgruntled customers were not an uncommon occurrence in the forging business. It seemed that every time some fool got arrested, they thought it was Phylo's fault. A few customers required firm convincing that his workmanship was first-rate and that he had actually done an excellent job. The thirty-eight Smith and Wesson revolver he kept in a holster nailed underneath the workbench was usually quite efficient at convincing even the angriest clients.

The vicious looking tommy gun pointed square at Phylo's middle, however, caused him to delay reaching for his pistol and give diplomacy a try.

"Gentlemen," Phylo said agreeably. "I'm sure we can settle any differences we may have quite amiably. If you will just let me know what the problem is, I'll see what I can do to set things straight."

The taller of the two intruders, a man who appeared to be in his forties with cold, ice-blue eyes, grinned evilly. "Norton, *we're* the ones who's gonna set things straight.

You gave Mister Capone some bad information that caused him to send a great deal of money to a politician who won't return it. The boss says he can't whack a thieving politician, but he *can* whack you for causin' him the loss."

Phylo froze, as a feeling like a cold straight razor being slowly drawn down his spine coursed through his being. "I told Capone the straight scoop on Pat Gunn. He's in New Mexico, like I said."

The tall man shook his head as he nodded to the greasy haired kid holding the submachine gun. "No one out there's ever heard of this Gunn fellow. You should've stayed a petty crook an' not gone and messed with Mister Capone. He wants us to make you into a good lesson to keep other folks from takin' advantage of his kind and trusting nature."

"I'll pay him back!" Phylo Norton screamed seconds before the tommy gun began spitting lead. The first three or four bullets stung like angry hornets. After that, he didn't feel a thing.

"Never before in all my born days, have I seen so blame many men working, and trucks roaring by without so much as a single soul dropping in for a drink. It just ain't normal," Fred Chapman sighed and took another swig of beer.

Woody watched a heavily loaded truck pulling a trailer rumble by the Bloated Goat. "That whole bunch is Mormons from Utah." He shook his head sadly. "Ain't nothing normal about them folks. They're even more God-happy than Baptists. Neither of 'em will risk taking a drink for fear of going to hell."

"They sure work like ants," Carla said. "From sunrise until it's too dark to work, there's a steady stream of trucks leaving here loaded with scrap iron."

Fred snorted. "Hard work's a curse on people who don't drink. Give me a drunk, lazy sinner any day. Besides, Mormons or any other kind of zealots make me downright nervous."

Woody could not help but worry what Wisdom would be like after the last truck had hauled the last load of scrap iron over Angel's Roost Pass. While the Mormons did not stop in the saloon, they were working, making noise; something was happening.

Once the mines were gutted, the town would become submerged in silence. With gasoline becoming rationed to four gallons a week, people who lived in the area would be forced to stay put.

Silence and death went hand-in-hand.

"I'm getting plenty worried about Pat Gunn," Irene said, twirling a full glass of mint julep. For the past few days she had been too unsettled to enjoy drinking. "The man's been gone for over two weeks now."

"There's a good dozen light bulbs burned out on that marquee of his," Fred commented. "If Pat's planning to actually show that movie he keeps advertising, now would seem like a good time to do it. Mormons might not have anything against W. C. Fields."

Woody nearly choked on his beer. "Fred, I never suspected you of being a knucklehead, until now. The way all religious fruitcakes makes rules is simple. If it feels good, or it's fun, it's a sin. And you'll go to Hell if you do it. Going to a moving picture show is most likely just as sinful as visiting a whorehouse, according to the book of Mormonitis."

Carla caused a blush to cross her husband's face when she said, "In my experience, Mormons are a horny lot. Generally, they wait until they're quite a distance from home to prove it. If Pearl's joint was open, I'd expect there'd be a lot of rattling going on from headboards banging the wall."

Irene endeared herself to Woody by changing the subject. "I wonder," she said, "how Pearl's doing. Nobody's seen her leave the Happy Eagle since she locked the front door and turned out the bar lights."

Spinner Olsson wheezed. "Pearl's sweet on Pat Gunn. I'd reckon she's up there pining away." The old man coughed and cleared his throat with a gulp of beer and continued. "Those hired killers have surely went and done ol' Pat in. That's too bad. I was hoping they'd come back asking questions again. I could use another five-spot."

Fred Chapman shook his head sadly as he stood. "I don't know how you got an idea caught in that noggin of yours that anybody's out to get Pat, let alone professional killers. I've known Pat for years and can't fathom why anyone would pay good money to have him shot. Pat Gunn owns a moving picture theater, for Pete's sake."

Spinner's silver dollar pealed like a fine church bell when he tossed it onto the bar. "If'n Pat shows up and still has a pulse, I'd reckon I'm wrong. In the meantime, get me another glass of beer while you're up."

Fred went and grabbed three frosty brown bottles of Carling Black Label beer from the dwindling supply in the cooler, one each for Woody, Carla and himself. He popped the tops, set them on the bar, filled Spinner's glass, then took his usual seat on a wobbly stool behind the counter.

Carla Johnson waited until the din of a passing diesel truck had faded to speak. "I'm hoping Pat gets back real soon. Pearl's most likely beside herself with worry. She's never admitted it, but she's in love with that man. The way things are going for her, she'd be crushed if something has happened to him."

Woody gave a dismissive shrug. "I can't figure out why folks hereabout are getting into a dither over a grown man taking off on a fishing trip. It's a lot lower in elevation on the Gila and a sight warmer than Wisdom. Even a man who doesn't like to fish can enjoy a pretty stream of water and a better climate for a spell."

"I'm gonna call that nasty sheriff," Irene said firmly. "I'm going to ask him if he's found out anything about who shot that arson investigator and if he's heard a thing about Pat Gunn. Our votes count from up here same as those in Silver City do."

"There's droves more voters down there, dear," Fred said sadly. "All of the voters left in Wisdom could barely make up a game of poker."

"I'm still going to call and yell at that sheriff," Irene affirmed. "He has it coming."

"Slow Ron's got the closest phone," Woody said. "The Jordans have one, but they've been keeping to themselves ever since we spread their boy's ashes off Angel's Roost Peak."

Spinner said, "Having to bury your kid is an awful thing."

"Pearl's got a phone," Carla said, looking out the window. "I don't think she would mind if we went to see how she's getting along."

Woody did not want his bride to ever again venture into a whorehouse, be it open or closed. He sipped at his beer while trying to come up with a solid reason to stay put.

Fred Chapman nodded toward Bowdrie's gas station. "Ron and Minnie's still out of town, from the looks of things. That old Moon car of theirs been gone for three or four days now. I hope the docs haven't put Slow Ron back in the hospital."

"Naw," Spinner said. "Minnie told us they sold the place. Maybe they've up and moved already. Ron wasn't hurt all that bad."

Irene shook her head. "The lights have been turned on and off in their living quarters. Somebody's home for sure. I'm going over there and bang on the door. I want to give that sheriff a piece of my mind."

Fred paid his wife no attention. He was staring through the front window, his wrinkled face a mask of utter astonishment. "Well, I'll be dipped. There's Slow Ron himself, standing outside looking around like a bull hit in the head with a sledgehammer."

"Good to hear he's back to normal," Woody said, jumping off his barstool to join in the rush to Bowdrie's Standard Oil Station.

CHAPTER TWENTY-EIGHT

"Now we know who shot Officer Frank Keller and it's someone we never suspected." Sheriff Sinrod sighed, stretched across his cluttered desk and handed the typewritten letter to Doctor Whitlock. "This turn of events clears Pat Gunn, but I have the sinking feeling he's already dead. Those state boys weren't here to investigate a cop's murder, they were here to hit Gunn; Keller's death was simply a handy coincidence."

The coroner muttered something unintelligible as he moved the letter into better light. His mouth dropped as he read the letter.

November 13th, 1942

Dear Sheriff Sinrod,

I am writing you this letter only to clear Mr. Pat Gunn of any wrongdoing in the matter of the slaying of Officer Frank Keller. I pulled the trigger that caused the arson investigator's demise.

Years of suffering abuse and beatings at the hands of my husband proved more than I could endure. Over a period of weeks, I made several trips to the abandoned mine that looks down on the highway. You see, I had determined my only way out was to shoot him with his own gun.

Courage, Sheriff, is something that I sadly lack, or I would have killed that man years ago.

The day I knew my husband would be driving back to

town on that road, I drank too much brandy to calm my frayed nerves. Unfortunately for Officer Keller, I mistook him for Marshal Ronald Bowdrie, my husband.

I am now many miles from Wisdom on my way to a new life. I wish to thank the good doctors in Silver City for giving out such wonderfully strong painkillers. Ronald was so drugged he never suspected he had signed deeds to the station, along with checks to close all of the bank accounts. I leave him homeless, penniless, without a car and with only one eye to make his way through life.

I did not kill Ronald Bowdrie, but all things considered, I feel the score is somewhat evened.

CATCH ME IF YOU CAN!
Signed,
Minnie S. Bowdrie

CHAPTER TWENTY-NINE

Coroner Whitlock snapped his mouth shut, stunned by the blunt coldness of what he had read. He cleared his throat. "A wise man once wrote, 'Hell hath no fury like a woman scorned' I suspect Ron Bowdrie missed reading it. Now that Minnie Bowdrie's confessed and headed for parts unknown in a Moon automobile, I'd venture she's hell on wheels, too."

Sam Sinrod's features remained frozen. He leaned back and laced his fingers behind his head. "Mrs. Bowdrie stood out like plain white wallpaper. I honestly can say that I'm going to have a hard time describing her for the wanted posters."

"The marshal likely has some pictures of her that he'll have no more use for." Doctor Whitlock lit a cigarette. "We have to go visit Bowdrie, tell him what's happened and show him the letter. Damn it, Sam, I feel somewhat responsible. I'm the reason he got all of those barbiturates."

"Bowdrie's lucky to be alive. If he hadn't been so blotto he didn't know what was going on, she'd have bumped him off. A few more of those pills would have done the trick. And probably not raised anyone's suspicions."

"You're right about that. A patient suffering intense pain can often forget taking a dose, or even two. Minnie was without a doubt the last person on earth I would've suspected of any wrongdoing. She would have gotten away clean as a whistle. I really wonder why she didn't put Bowdrie six feet under, having such a golden opportunity."

"Because what she did do to him is worse. He's broke, humiliated and crippled. Ron Bowdrie will have a lot of hard years to remember back on how badly he treated his wife."

"I've a feeling Minnie would have made a peach of a mate. If Bowdrie hadn't been a peckerhead, none of this would have happened." Whitlock crushed out his cigarette. "Of course, if people used their heads for something besides hanging a hat on, you'd be out of a job."

"It'd be nice to live in a world that doesn't need lawmen, Doc. But we don't. I'm going to phone Santa Fe, tell the attorney general we've solved Keller's murder. I'm also going to pressure him about Pat Gunn. Tell him we have witnesses that saw Neto Diego and Garret Black take him away. If Gunn's still alive, which I doubt, maybe things will turn out."

Doctor Whitlock lowered his ahead. "I sure hope so." He turned to leave. At the doorway he hesitated long enough to softly utter, "Please, God, let him be safe."

Pearl Dunbar shook the grates on her coal-burning Wehrle range. Then, using a poker, scraped out a few clinkers from among the glowing coals. She added a half-dozen fist-sized lumps of coal and closed the firebox.

It took several minutes before Pearl had the draft doors and damper adjusted just so to hold an oven temperature of three-hundred-fifty degrees.

Today she was baking two loaves of honey wheat bread that she had made from scratch. Yesterday it had been rhubarb pies prepared from a large rhubarb plant behind the bar that had somehow been sheltered enough to escape being frozen. The day before that, she had spent all day slow-cooking a beef roast smothered in onions, potatoes, carrots and burgundy wine.

Any type of work to keep her mind busy was what she strove for. It was no good, however. Every waking moment, Pearl fretted over the safety of her beloved Pat Gunn.

Many times she had called her father, the governor, to ask why her love had not been returned to her. Pearl would have kept to her word never to call him again, if he had honored his promises. All her persistent phone calling had accomplished was to upset the old windbag's secretary, who curtly reiterated time and again that, "The governor is on vacation in the Bahamas and will be incommunicado for at least another week, possibly longer."

Pearl chided herself for ever trusting any politician, especially when it was her own father.

If anything happens to Pat Gunn, I'll visit every major newspaper and radio station in New Mexico. When I'm through telling the truth, ex-Governor Herschell Castle won't be able to get elected dog catcher of lower little Chilie, wherever the hell that podunk town is.

She reflected on her thoughts and realized no town could possibly be worse off than what Wisdom had become. Aside from listening to bad war news on the single radio station she could receive and Nero's occasional cussing and squawking, the once bustling gold mining center had become silent as the inside of a tomb. Except, that is, for the noise created by the scrap iron men who were rapidly tearing down and hauling away Wisdom's sole reason for being. After they were finished, silence would reign in this canyon as it had for centuries before.

When word had first come out about the mines closing, Pearl had known she would leave here with nothing but her beloved Cord automobile, some clothes and the parrot. The Happy Eagle Bar and the acre of land on which it stood were all but valueless. Once Pearl Dunbar drove her shiny green Cord over Angel's Roost Pass, there would be no reason to ever look back. The problem was, she was chained here by her heartstrings. Pat Gunn had become the center of her universe, her reason for being. And he was in terrible trouble.

Pearl, for what was likely the twentieth time today, went to the front window and stared down the lonely, forlorn gravel road that ran alongside of the purling waters of Midas Creek. In the distance she saw only an empty truck leaving a dust cloud as it headed to the Hidden Treasure Mine.

After a long moment, Pearl daubed a tear from a leaky eye using a corner of her print apron. The bread needed checking. Baking anything in this high altitude demanded her full attention. She sighed at the silent canyon, turned and strode to the kitchen.

"Our town has died around us, Mama." Oliver Jordan draped a sheltering blanket over his wife's frail shoulders.

"And the undertaker's taking away the body, one small piece at a time," Harriet said. Her small voice was strong this crisp, sunny, windless afternoon.

The old couple sat on the porch of their small home sipping hot chocolate, watching throngs of men systematically remove buildings and machinery from the Hidden Treasure Mine.

"I worked there all of my life," Oliver said, blowing white tendrils of steam from his cup. "Everyone always thought that mine would run for a hundred years."

Harriet's rheumy eyes focused on the craggy spire of Angel's Roost mountain. "Everything and everyone dies, Papa, even towns and mines."

"I know, dear," Oliver said, gently stroking his wife's silver hair with the back of his hand. "But it hurts, just the same."

CHAPTER THIRTY

"But I own this place," Ronald Bowdrie kept whining mechanically over and over to the skinny, hatchet-faced, middle-aged man wearing a natty pinstripe suit who claimed to be Rufus Talbot, a lawyer from Silver City.

It had been Talbot's persistent banging on the door that had roused Bowdrie. The lawyer had parked his Chrysler Airflow Sedan on the opposite side of the gas station where the entourage from the Bloated Goat could not see it until they were standing in front of the building.

"Simmer down, Slow—uh, Ron," Woody said, eyeing the stranger. "Let the man say his piece, even if he is an idiot."

Talbot glared at the scruffy old miner. "An insult will not accomplish anything, my dear sir, except to raise the ire of a man who is a new neighbor."

"What's an ire?" Spinner gasped. The burst of speed he had put on to reach the station had used up nearly all of his wind.

Fred Chapman said, "Irish word. It means pissed off."

"Those people *are* always ones to fight," Carla added.

"I didn't sell my place to anyone," Ron Bowdrie said simply.

The lawyer opened a leather valise, took out a couple of legal-looking pieces of paper and held them up to Bowdrie's good eye. "You will observe, sir, *your* notarized signature along with that of your wife's on these recorded deeds which legally conveyed to me all of the land and buildings you own in Wisdom, along with their contents."

"But I didn't sell nothing to nobody," Bowdrie repeated more loudly. Anger was burning away the drugs. "You're a damn liar!"

Rufus Talbot sighed. "Your wife mentioned several times your memory had been impaired by the terrible incident that destroyed your eye. I assure you, Mister Bowdrie, I paid the sum of three hundred dollars cash money for this gas station and home. This is a substantial risk in such a town as Wisdom. Perhaps, I should have Sheriff Sinrod come and explain the law to you."

"Minnie," Ron yelled sharply into the open front door. "Get your lazy butt out here and straighten this man out!"

Woody cocked his head to the vacant space where the Moon automobile had always been parked. "Ron, I think your wife might have gone somewhere in the car. Maybe she left three—four days ago."

The lawyer said, "If you are referring to a 1926 Moon Diana, I notarized the title into the name of Minnie Bowdrie in front of Mister Bowdrie. At the time he also authorized the closing of all of their bank accounts and even cashed in a substantial life insurance policy he thoughtfully carried on himself for the wife's benefit."

"Minnie!" Bowdrie screamed again into the open door. Only stone silence answered. "Minnie." He was sobbing now as stark realization of what had happened crashed past the last of the Phenobarbital. Ron Bowdrie wailed over and over, "Oh Minnie, please don't do this to me."

Talbot's voice was soft when he said to Bowdrie, "I'm very sorry your wife isn't about. Perhaps she will return shortly." A look of puzzlement crossed the lawyer's stern face. "Mrs. Bowdrie was quite plain about being moved out before now. Legally, I have had possession of this property for five days. I really can't explain why your wife has not moved you out as agreed."

"Minnie's up and left him for beating on her," Woody said plainly. "That's the simple gist of the matter."

Ron Bowdrie dropped to his knees. His face was beet red as he screamed and cried at the same time. "Oh Minnie, I'm so sorry. I'll never hit you again. I promise."

Lawyer Talbot returned the deeds to his valise with a snort. "Martial discord does not enter into my legally purchasing this property." He turned to the shaking Bowdrie. "I expect you to leave the premises, forthwith."

The marshal stood and choked back a sob. "Everything I own is here: tools, air compressor, cans of oil, furniture. There's almost a thousand gallons of gasoline in the tanks."

"Correction, Mister Bowdrie." The lawyer's voice turned icy. "You mean *I* own. To be agreeable, you may take your clothes, but I want you gone before nightfall. I hold no sympathy for a wife beater."

Spinner shuffled to Ron's side. "I'll help him move out. There's an extra room in my cabin going to waste. Reckon it'd be nice to have someone around to help keep the fires going."

"Carla and me'll help move Ron's stuff," Woody said. "It's not a far piece to carry things."

Fred Chapman looked at his wife. "Business being slow as it is, I suppose we can help, too."

"And I will make certain only personal belongings are taken," Talbot said firmly. "Before I leave here today, I shall padlock everything."

"Then we had better get to cracking," Woody said, glaring at the lawyer.

Spinner placed a hand on Marshal Bowdrie's quivering shoulder and ushered the sobbing man inside to glean what he could from the ashes of a love he had turned to hate by his own fists.

A tangerine moon was floating high in a back sea of twinkling stars over the City of Santa Fe. Lieutenant Neto Diego stared at it with stern, angry eyes through a window of their suite in the Adobe Walls Hotel.

"The boss finally heard from the governor," Neto said to his partner several minutes after hanging up the phone. "The news is not good. Not good at all."

Garret Black poured whiskey into a glass with a raw egg and a dash of hot sauce in it. "I really want to whack Pat Gunn. No one has ever run up such a bill on room service as he has. That man must have a hollow leg. It'll be the very devil trying to explain how we let something like this happen."

"I want to kill him, too," Neto said sadly. "I really do."

"I'd rub him out for free," Black growled. "Well, almost for free anyway. I do have a reputation to uphold."

"We must do what we are ordered," Neto sighed. "As I said, the news is not good."

Sergeant Black swirled the egg and whiskey around in his glass. "Do you mean not good news for us, or not good news for that spendthrift, Gunn?"

Neto Diego returned to looking at the moon. "Somehow, some way, that gluttonous fool has gained the personal protection of Governor Castle. If Pat Gunn suffers so much as a scratch, we will be guarding crosswalks for school children."

"Well, that's a fine turn of events. First we're sent to whack him. Then we have to haul him to a fancy hotel, feed and protect him. Then he turns out to be good buddies with the governor. I tell you, Neto, I'm retiring and moving to Montana."

"I may join you there if the quality of our government does not improve." Neto Diego brightened. "It just struck me that our esteemed boss, whose name you shall never mention, told me that Gunn may now be returned home. He did not order us to drive him there."

"Perhaps we could give him a lift for *part* of the way."

"Sergeant," Lieutenant Diego said cheerfully, "you are reading my mind."

Beneath the same colorful moon that had held Neto Diego's attention, Woody Johnson and Carla backed their Model A truck up to the hand-operated gas pump at what was now lawyer Rufus Talbot's Standard Oil Station.

Woody climbed out, fished a pair of bolt cutters from among the clutter of empty metal containers they had brought along for the occasion. A quick snip and the cheap lock securing the crank to the pump was history.

Removing gasoline from a shyster's tank who had filched it himself in the first place, wasn't the same as stealing. Not by a long shot. Any fool knew gasoline went bad if kept long in storage.

It took a few hours of cranking the pump, filling containers and running back and forth to the cabin. But by the time a red sun was winking over the eastern peaks, the couple had laid away an impressive supply of gasoline to help them face the hardships of rationing.

CHAPTER THIRTY-ONE

Pat Gunn had never thought much about turkeys—until now. They were stupid, noisy, and most of all, smelly. The more he studied the birds in the rear view mirror, the more they resembled buzzards. Every time the drunk, foul-mouthed driver of the battered old Dodge truck slammed on the brakes, a renewed din of gobbling, squawking, along with clouds of feathers arose from the hundreds of birds contained in the bed of the truck by a covering of chicken wire.

"A few more stops, *señor,*" Lito Jiminez, the driver said, grabbing up the bottle of mescal from the seat between them. "Then I shall leave you where the road turns off to Wisdom. I sold more turkeys in Old Horse Springs than I would where you live. And only the Aragon family lives there."

"That will be fine," Pat answered, watching the pale gray worm inside the bottle swirl when Lito upended it and drank. He shivered when thoughts of the treacherous narrow mountain road from where they were, just outside of Reserve to the turnoff at Alma, crossed his mind. Being drunk would take a lot of the terror out of the switchbacks. But he had no money and Lito did appear inclined to offer to share his mescal.

"I'm thankful for the ride," Pat said.

"De nada, señor. It is almost Thanksgiving, then *Navidad.* A damn fine time for *fiesta."*

Pat nodded sullenly, hunkered down in the seat and remembered back on the strange manner in which those two state policeman had turned on him. And they had been so friendly up until the time Sergeant Black had rudely grabbed him by the collar of his coat and forcibly removed him from the Packard. Then Black had painfully kicked him into the barrow ditch before the pair sped away, laughing.

Pat had thought it odd the police were driving him home by way of Magdalena. That road received very little traffic and was much rougher than going through Silver City. Then, miles from any sign of civilization, Garret Black and Neto Diego's pleasant disposition had turned downright ugly for no reason he could fathom.

All lawmen, Pat decided, were not to be trusted.

The fact they had thrown him out penniless was the cruelest blow of all. When Pat had mentioned this fact, Lieutenant Diego had nastily growled something about a two-hundred-and-eighty-dollar room service bill, just before he jammed down the accelerator and showered him with flying gravel.

On the good side, both policemen had made it plain that no one was out to do him harm and the shooting of Officer Keller had been solved when Marshal Bowdrie's wife confessed to the crime. Al Capone, they added with a grunt, would not be bothering him in the future.

Pat had a difficult time trying to understand why Minnie Bowdrie would want to go and shoot an arson investigator. Being married to Slow Ron, however, would be enough to cause most anyone to lose her mind. Anyway, Pearl and Woody would explain everything once he was home.

It would be wonderful to see Pearl again, but the nine-mile walk over Angel's Roost Pass was a good deal farther than he'd ever hiked before. Perhaps he could catch a ride with the mail carrier or somebody going to Wisdom. At the very least, Pearl's velvety soft hands giving him a much needed backrub afterwards would make for a welcome homecoming.

"Oh *señor,*" Lito grinned, handing Pat the nearly empty mescal bottle that still contained the worm. "Drink these, *gusano.* It will help bring a smile to the lady's face."

Pat cocked a suspicious eye at the shriveled gray grub. There appeared to be sufficient mescal remaining to make the task worthwhile.

"Salud," Pat said as he brought the bottle to his lips, tipped it and yearned to be home in Wisdom.

When the huge Cummins diesel truck pulling a long flatbed trailer rumbled over the summit of Angel's Roost Pass, Pat Gunn was astonished by what he saw. The changes that had been wrought at the Hidden Treasure mine site during his absence were stupefying. Where before metal-covered buildings had sprawled across the mountainside, there were now only bare steel beams pointing skyward, like sun-bleached rib bones of some great and ancient creature that had died, eons past.

"You men have been busy," Pat said to the young driver who wore a perpetual smile and had been kind enough to stop and offer him a ride before he had walked a hundred feet.

"My dear sir," the driver said, "idle hands are the Devil's playground." He reached into the glove box and extracted a few pamphlets. "Take and read these, friend. They explain the true word of God. They will give you guidance to avoid the punishing, though cleansing, fires of Hell."

Pat forced a smile as he took the brochures and tucked them into a jacket pocket. He had spent more than twenty hours riding with a drunken, turkey-hauling madman over narrow mountain roads, he had slugged down a worm and eaten Doctor Whitlock's pork liver and rutabagas. Hell didn't seem much of a threat.

"Thanks for giving me a lift," Pat said.

"I hope you'll get some good out of the literature I gave you."

"Oh, I'm certain I will." Pat breathed a sigh of relief when the flashing lights of the Starlight Theater marquee came into view. "I'll read them the first chance I get."

Almost in front of the Bloated Goat Saloon, another huge truck, this one loaded heavy and high with untold tons of greasy machinery, roared down the canyon toward them. The driver nonchalantly pulled over, almost into Midas Creek, stopping to the sibilant sound of air brakes.

The monstrous truck thundered past, missing them by scant inches.

After a moment Pat had regained enough breath to say, "I'll get out here. I own that moving picture theater. I also need to drop into the saloon to let folks know I'm back."

The young Mormon had concern etched into his face as he once again reached into the glove box. "You had better have these pamphlets, too. I sincerely hope you will take the message to heart and avoid the terrible fate that awaits unbelievers."

"Thanks again for the ride," Pat said, scooping up the stack of brochures.

"May God have mercy on your soul," the unnamed driver said over the hiss of air brakes. Then he was gone in a cloud of dust.

"I think the Almighty just did," Pat beamed when, through the front window of the Bloated Goat Saloon, he caught a glimpse of the most beautiful redheaded lady in Wisdom smiling back at him.

Then Pat saw the sheriff's cruiser parked alongside the bar. "Heaven and Hell, Hell and Heaven. It seems you just can't have one without the other." He clucked his tongue and headed for the front door.

In downtown Fresno, California, at a used car part supplier's lot across from rows of raisin warehouses, the unkempt proprietor kicked a tire dismissively.

"Moons ain't very valuable cars, Ma'am." The man chewed on a stub of cigar while paying more attention to the woman's cleavage than the automobile she was attempting to sell.

"My husband told me the very same thing," Minnie said, causing the cigar to droop.

"Selling it off for parts might make me a little profit."

Minnie Bowdrie, now going by the name of Lola Sweet, thought, *It's good no one ever applies for a license plate for parts, just the whole car.*

"You got the title?"

The pretty blonde with short curly hair and red pouty lips fished it from her purse and handed it over. "You will notice the person my husband got it from for a bad debt has signed it over."

"Just a formality Ma'am, the city makes us check is all." The greasy man barely glanced at the title, then studied the Moon Diana. "I'll go thirty dollars for it, just to help out a nice dame."

The lady by the name of Lola Sweet smiled coyly, took the proffered money, tucked it into her purse and began walking the short distance to the train depot. The weather in California was much more agreeable than it had been in the mountains of Wisdom. Once she had put a hundred miles or more distance between her and the only thing that could possibly be traced, she thought she might stay for awhile.

Whistling a tune popular a few years ago, "Cry Baby Cry," Lola walked along the sidewalk beneath towering palm trees until finally melting into the milling crowds.

CHAPTER THIRTY-TWO

Pat Gunn was taken aback by Pearl Dunbar being at the Bloated Goat, then more so when he swung the door open to become overwhelmed by her new appearance. The madam had bobbed her long red tresses to shoulder length. Instead of the usual revealing dress, Pearl sported a pair of skintight blue jeans along with a western shirt that fit well enough to make Pat wonder if she had been melted down, then poured into them.

The sweet smell of spring cherry blossoms was intoxicating as the angelic vision of loveliness gave a squeal of delight, ran happily into Pat's open arms and planted her lips to his in a deep, passionate kiss.

Woody Johnson said from a barstool, "I'd reckon we're all glad to see you, Pat, but Pearl's showing it more than the rest of us are gonna do."

Pat gently pulled away from luscious ruby lips, but kept his gaze fixed on Pearl's emerald eyes. "I'm mighty glad to be home. This has been a strange past few weeks. I heard Minnie Bowdrie killed that cop, and from the looks of things, Lonnie Dillman's gone and hired a drove of Mormons to work for him."

Sheriff Sam Sinrod and Doctor Whitlock sat at a table drinking beer.

"You're a lucky man," Sinrod said to Pat. "The attorney general phoned a couple of days ago to tell us the state police had you under protective custody. With Officer Keller's murder solved, they were bringing you home. I suspect

Lieutenant Diego and Sergeant Black didn't quite do what they were supposed to do."

Pat shrugged. "Well, they mostly treated me okay, but they sure are unpredictable." He rubbed a hand over a scraggly beard. "I could use some scrubbing up. I'm also surprised you came all the way up here to meet me."

Doctor Whitlock drank a swallow of beer and said, "We're actually here to investigate the supposed theft of gasoline from Bowdrie's old Standard Oil Station. Also, we needed to question the marshal about where his wife might've gone. She didn't leave us a lot to go on."

The sheriff said, "The marshal seems totally stunned by the turn of events. He admits to beating his wife, but can't make the connection with why she tried to kill him. Her shooting the officer doesn't upset him near as much as her leaving him broke. Anyway, Minnie Bowdrie's long gone. That Moon car stands out. When it turns up, we'll have her."

Woody snorted. "There likely never was but a dab of gas in that tank. I'm betting what little was there went and evaporated. That lawyer's nothing but a sorehead."

"Dry climate up here," Carla added.

Spinner wheezed. "Slow Ron's living with me now that his wife went and sold the joint out from under him. He's taking it hard. Mostly all he does is sit an' read the Bible."

"I've got some pamphlets he can have," Pat said, giving Pearl a squeeze. "I think I'd like a whiskey and hailstones to drink while folks fill me in on what all has happened here while I've been gone."

"Plan on having a couple, sweetie," Pearl cooed. "This will take a while. We'll start with your friend Woody and Carla getting married."

Pat Gunn wondered if two drinks were going to be enough.

CHAPTER THIRTY-THREE

December 24, 1942

Sparse, fluffy flakes of snow were drifting gently earthward from a pewter sky when Doctor Whitlock pulled his sleek 90 series Cadillac to a stop beside the Starlight Theater. He immediately hopped out, opened an umbrella and ushered Penelope Leathers across the light dusting of snow that had accumulated and into the warm and cheery lobby. Sam Sinrod climbed out alone, struggling with a pair of heavy bags that he held tight as he dashed to be out of the cold.

"I'm glad you folks could make it," Pat Gunn said happily as Pearl and he came to greet the new arrivals. "The pass was iced up bad, I'd imagine."

"No," Whitlock replied. "The sun was shining and the road's dry right up until we dropped over Angel's Roost. This storm's only here."

"The great weather's what keeps me around these parts," Spinner Olsson wheezed as he shuffled over to take Penelope's wrap. He was obviously taken aback by seeing another woman taunt tradition by wearing slacks, but he kept quiet about the matter.

Doctor Whitlock proudly began introducing his lovely date to the others in attendance, while Sam Sinrod handed the heavy bags he carried to Pat Gunn.

"I brought along some bratwurst for the potluck dinner," Sam said. "They're a tad heavy on the garlic for my taste but I think most folks will enjoy them."

Pat began laying out the already cooked sausage in a large metal pan where they could be warmed later. The sheriff hung up his coat and came to help.

"Nice of you to bring in a moving picture and show it for free. It was also good of you to invite Doc and me," Sam said, staring blackly at the sausage. "*Never Give a Sucker an Even Break* just came out last year. This must be costing plenty." He decided not to mention the word 'sucker' on the flashing marquee was still misspelled.

"Well," Pat shrugged. "People here had to deal with quite a setback when the mines closed. I think we could all use some cheering up with what all's gone on lately. Pearl's loaned me the money until my insurance check comes through."

Sam cocked and eye and smiled. "I sent a letter to the insurance commissioner, verifying your house fire wasn't of suspicious origin. There shouldn't be any problems."

A chorus of feminine "oohs" and "ahs" from across the lobby took their attention.

"Doc Whitlock bought his girl an engagement ring with a diamond in it big enough to choke a goat." The sheriff spoke with a hint of longing. "I never saw a man fall so hard for a dame. I just hope he's fallen in love instead of lust, but he's sure falling hard, wherever he lands."

"Pretty lady," Pat commented. "This marrying thing is becoming an epidemic. First Woody comes down with it and hitches up with Carla. Then the Doc catches whatever's going around. I plan to pop the question to Pearl myself, when I can afford to buy her a ring. She'd loan me the money, but that wouldn't seem right, somehow."

"Women can be fickle about things like that."

Pat gave an adoring glance to his love. "Pearl is a beautiful lady, isn't she? And I have to admire the way she stood by me when things were looking bleak."

"Pearl Dunbar likely helped you out more than we'll ever know."

"You and Doc Whitlock did your best for me, too. That's why I wanted you folks to join us here at the Starlight this afternoon. W. C. Fields is great in this film. He plays a really bad writer trying to pawn off a terrible movie script on a studio."

"Let's hope it's not based on a true story," Sam commented wryly.

Both men turned to watch as Ron Bowdrie came out, grabbed a bottle of Coca-Cola along with a small sack of popcorn, then returned to the dark of the theater without saying a word to anyone.

"Bowdrie's head must've gotten warped more than anyone thought," said Pat. "I should hate that man, but I don't. Actually, I feel sorry for him and what he's become. He's lost a good fifty pounds because Spinner says he refuses to eat. I hear all Ron does these days is sit and stare out a window or read the Bible. The eye patch Spinner made for him out of an old belt keeps him from looking too spooky. I sure thought he'd be coming out of it by now."

"The shard of glass damaged only his eye. Minnie shattered his pride. She also made him look like a fool. It was just more than the man could deal with."

Pat eyed the tempting trays of fried chicken, mashed potatoes with gravy, vegetables, pies and cakes along with homemade bread and a mountain of sausage. He draped a covering towel over the bratwurst to keep them from drying out.

"Any news on Minnie?" Pat asked, tucking the edges of towel tight underneath the pan.

Sheriff Sinrod shook his head. "Not a word. The longer

it takes to catch a criminal, the more likely it is they'll get away. If she *is* caught, they'll put her in the electric chair. That would be a terrible cloud to live under."

Pat continued down the row of trays, checking on the food. An enshrouding somber cast covered his usually happy face. "Minnie was married to Slow Ron for eleven years. I'm sorry about that officer being shot, but I really do hope you never catch her."

Sheriff Sinrod sighed. "I'll do my job when and if, but I'm not going to push the matter. A woman who's been beaten as much as that poor soul likely was, deserves to fly free."

"Well, it's out of our hands." A familiar smile blossomed on the theater owner's visage. "We're here to forget our problems, along with those of the world for a while. There's nothing like a moving picture to make that happen. And W. C. Fields is always a hoot."

"I saw *The Bank Dick* a couple of years ago." Sam rolled his eyes to Penelope, who was snuggled close to Bryce Whitlock's side. "I had a girl back then, and took her to see it. Linda Powers was her name. Being sheriff is a full-time job. I suppose I didn't give her the attention she deserved. Anyway, she wound up married to a clerk at the hardware store, has her second child on the way."

"The way this epidemic's going, you'll find yourself a gem of a dame right soon. Remember, the keepers have a tendency to come along when you least expect them."

Sam started to say something, only to sputter into muteness when Pearl stepped over, pointing to the wall clock. The ex-madam had chosen one of her more revealing green dresses to wear for the occasion. One furtive glance at Pearl's divine cleavage had once again silenced the sheriff.

"Excuse me, dear," Pearl said sweetly. "It's time for you

to start the movie. If people are going to be able to eat supper at six, we can't begin late. It will take time to reheat some of the food."

"I'll get the film running and in focus," Pat said, gently grasping Pearl's hand. "Then I'll pop down and watch it with you."

"I'd like that."

"Folks," Pat shouted loudly enough to quiet conversations. "It's time to take your seats for the show. I hope you'll enjoy it. There likely won't be another until after the war's over."

Numerous, familiar voices thanked Pat Gunn as they filed through the wide doors to sparsely fill the Starlight Theater, for what would be the last moving picture that would ever play in Wisdom, New Mexico.

At this point we shall take our leave of the remote mountain town, while laughter still echoes from the craggy cliffs of Angel's Roost Canyon. The marquee lights of the Starlight Theater are flashing a beacon of welcome relief from the raging storms of war, in a world gone mad.

Inside the cozy Starlight Theater, each person is surviving the only way he or she knows how, making the best of each day as it comes.

CHAPTER THIRTY-FOUR

Four months later, when the snows of winter begin to melt on Angel's Roost Mountain, Pat Gunn will be forced to accept the futility of his vigil and extinguish the marquee lights on his beloved Starlight Theater for the final time.

Pearl Dunbar and he will leave the town of Wisdom, never to return. Those who remain shall either drift away or become interred in a decaying cemetery, beneath the scars of an abandoned gold mine.

Vandals and weather, along with the occasional fire started by lightning or a careless camper, will conspire to reduce this once proud boom city of the mountains to crumbling stone foundations, overgrown with brush and weeds.

The town of Wisdom is resigned to exist only in faded photographs or the impersonal pages of history books.

The dreams of generations are now dust upon cold earth.

And the dreamers, dust beneath.

Dust into dust, and under dust, to lie,
Sans wine, sans song, sans singer,
and—sans end.

Omar Khayyàm—Rubaiyat